Window to Danger

Window to Danger

What would you do if you witnessed a murder but no one believed you?

That's the position Desiree "Dizzy" Foster finds herself in. Through a bedroom window, she watched as her neighbor strangled a woman. But when the police arrive, there's no body and no evidence. They're not buying her story because she has a reputation in Tremont for being a little different, a little strange. She might be both of those things but she's definitely not a liar. She knows what she saw.

Easton Anderson is a man who is comfortable with numbers and logic. He doesn't believe in healing crystals, Tarot cards, or aura cleansing. So when Dizzy says she witnessed a murder, he wants to believe her. He truly does. But it isn't easy.

But the more time he spends with Dizzy, the more he gets pulled into the mystery. Something is going on next door, and if she's right, there's a murderer living only a few feet away. He'll have to trust more than the figures on his spreadsheets if he's going to keep the woman he's falling in love with from becoming the next victim.

Window to Danger

Danger Incorporated

Book Seven

BY

OLIVIA JAYMES

www.OliviaJaymes.com

WINDOW TO DANGER
Copyright © 2017 by Olivia Jaymes
Print Edition

Chapter One

I T HAD BEEN a long day and an even longer week but the moon was full and the weather mild. A perfect evening for Desiree "Dizzy" Foster to do a little yoga and meditation by moonlight. There was an energy in the air during the full moon that was absent at any other time. It was almost magical.

More mundane was Dizzy's summer job volunteering at the community center giving art lessons to children and adults. She loved opening up the world of art to her students, but today hadn't gone well from practically the moment she'd opened her eyes. The alarm clock hadn't gone off and she'd been running late for the rest of the day, constantly trying to catch up. She deserved a glass of wine with her dinner. Maybe two.

"I have all week to work in the studio," she told herself in the mirror as she tugged on her yoga pants and t-shirt before making a face at her reflection. "And I'll try that new cookie recipe too."

Teaching was wonderful but actually creating something with her own two hands was Dizzy's true passion. She'd known that she was destined to be an artist from a young age.

Pouring herself a glass of wine in the kitchen, Dizzy could see the full moon through the windows casting its light across her backyard despite the clouds that kept drifting in front of it. A frisson of excitement ran up her spine as she eased the back door open. The next half hour was *her* time. A little selfish but she didn't care. It was these moments that kept her sane when all hell seemed to have broken loose in her too busy life.

When Dizzy had been a chubby child of only four or five, her mother Tami had taught her the Moon Salutations, so different than the Sun Salutations that she'd learned at first. As Tami had patiently helped her learn each pose she'd told Dizzy how the moon represented the mother and feminine yin. She'd spoken of how the moon brought cycles to their lives, invisible rhythms that people often ignored, but that didn't mean they weren't there. It had been a powerful lesson at a young age – not everything could be seen by the eyes. It was a lesson that some people never learned.

Of course, now Dizzy was all grown up and her parents Tamara and Louis were doing Sun and Moon Salutations in Greece at the moment while working on an archaeological dig. Some parents retired to Florida and played golf. Dizzy's parents traveled the world looking for adventure and spiritual harmony.

Slipping out to her back deck, Dizzy laid out the yoga mat and closed her eyes, taking several deep breaths, absorbing the moon's energy with each inhale and then exhaling the negative energy of the crappy day she'd had. The tension began to drain from her body and her senses came more alive. She was acutely aware of the rustle of each and every leaf on the trees in her backyard, the chirp of the cicadas, and the music of the cricket. The cool air ran across her skin, raising goosebumps.

Somewhere in the distance a dog barked as the scent of grass, earth, and flowers tickled her nostrils. Her lids fluttered open and she stared up at the purple night sky dotted with tiny stars. She'd gone to art school and college in New York and she'd missed the stars that had been dimmed by all the city lights. There had never been a question of her staying there. She'd been glad to come home where she could actually see the sky.

Placing her wine glass down beside her she stood in position on the back porch as the cares of the day slowly fell away. Slowly and deliberately, Dizzy moved through her yoga poses before finally sinking to a sitting position at the end, cross-legged on the mat. Smiling serenely, she gave the moon a playful wink, her mood happier than it had been in over twelve hours.

She took a sip of her wine, enjoying the fruity taste on her tongue, but her attention was snagged away as her neighbor turned on an upstairs light, the glow illuminating the inside of the house like a movie screen at the local theatre. A woman came into view in the window for a moment and then disappeared just as quickly. Dizzy had to blink a few times to make sure she hadn't imagined it.

Her new neighbor Trip Stanford must have company because Dizzy was quite sure the man lived in the house alone. A Tremont resident for the last five years or so, he'd moved in about three months ago and she'd taken over a bundt cake to welcome him to the block. He'd invited her in for some lemonade to go with the cake and they'd chatted about the weather but nothing of any consequence. He'd been friendly and charming but they hadn't had a conversation since, content to wave and smile when they saw one another. There hadn't been a woman in sight that day nor any day after. He appeared to live a quiet life which everyone appreciated, and better yet he kept his lawn mowed and his mailbox painted.

Rolling up her mat, Dizzy padded back into the house on bare feet as the air outside grew chillier despite the calendar on the wall. It said the end of July but it had been abnormally cool this summer, which the whole town was enjoying.

"Damn," she muttered under her breath as she tucked her mat behind the door, ready for another day. "Forgot my wine. I need that."

Dashing back to grab her glass, she saw the woman she'd seen earlier back in the window but this time Trip was there as well. He had bent his head low to her ear as if speaking urgently or persuasively but the woman was having none of it, shaking her head vehemently. She tried to move away but Trip caught her by the arm, jerking her back, but the female didn't give up trying to pull away. Before Dizzy could even take a breath, Trip had his hands around the woman's neck and all she could do was watch in horror, her heart racing as the poor woman clawed at Trip's fingers and then crumpled to the floor. The moment had played out like a horrific scene in an old time silent film but this was all too real.

At some point, Dizzy's hands had come up to cover her mouth but they needn't have bothered because her scream of terror was silent, clawing to get out of her tightly closed throat, but the only sound that was able to escape was a small squeak. She stood frozen for a moment, her limbs not taking any orders from her brain but then her body started to attention again as if she'd been hit by a stun gun. She stumbled back into her kitchen on trembling legs, flipping the lock closed behind her and falling to her knees as her legs gave way underneath her and hot tears pricked behind her eyes. Her breaths came in gasps and fits as she struggled to pull oxygen into her aching lungs.

With a grunt of effort, she propelled herself across her kitchen to the counter and grabbed the phone, fumbling to remember her passcode and unlock it. Dizzy's shaking hands were barely able to dial and it took several tries before the call connected.

"911, what's your emergency?"

"I need to report a murder."

Chapter Two

LEANING AGAINST THE makeshift bar in the Anderson building atrium, Easton Anderson poured himself another glass of wine and tried to pretend he was enjoying himself at this dead boring cocktail party. It was basically a business meeting pretending to be something fun and sociable but he wasn't fooled in the least. He wouldn't even be here if he wasn't the Chief Financial Officer of Anderson Industries but duty always came first. He'd learned that at his father's knee.

"You'd make a lousy actor."

Easton turned to see his cousin Leann, who had recently taken over the Human Resources department after living in Florida for several years. She looked ridiculously happy since falling in love with Zach Gibson. Leave it to the Andersons to keep it all in the family. Zach's sister Gigi was married to Leann's brother West.

"Then thank goodness I decided against that career on the stage," Easton smirked. "I'll have to make do as a financial genius."

"Modest too," his cousin sighed. "Seriously, you look like your cat died. Can you smile or something? We're celebrating closing a deal that's going to give you more money to count, Scrooge McDuck."

He should be happy. They'd signed a deal to build a housing development in a growing town about a hundred miles away. To thank the staff that had been working on the proposal night and day for months, they'd thrown this party.

"I am happy," he said automatically. "Another feather in the cap of Anderson Industries."

Leann shook her head. "You're not fooling anyone. You're miserable."

He might not be giddy as a schoolgirl with her first crush but he sure as hell wasn't miserable. What did she expect him to do?

"Just because I'm not dancing and singing around the room doesn't mean I'm unhappy. I'm thrilled we got the contract. This is going to create a lot of jobs in the area."

Which would probably get West re-elected as mayor whether he liked it or not. Even if he didn't run, his name would just be written in on the ballots by the voters.

Eyes narrowed, his pretty cousin was looking him up and down. "I stand by my assessment. You're not a happy man. And do you know why?"

If he didn't let her have her say she'd dog his heels until his last breath.

"No, but I know you're dying to tell me why so get on with it."

"Because you're alone," Leann said bluntly. "And if you don't do something about that soon you're going to grow into a crotchety old man that only cares about profit and loss state-ments and has a cash register for a heart. Is that what you want?

Because you're well on your way."

"I am not alone," Easton objected, his mind drifting to his most recent girlfriend. "I've been dating."

Snorting, Leann rolled her eyes. "How about we talk about the women you date? They're all boring as hell. Even you think so because I rarely hear that you've dated one more than a couple of times. Are you even dating anyone right now?"

"I've been seeing Melanie Elliott, a well-respected real estate attorney in town. As a matter of fact, she and I attended a dinner party a few nights ago."

The actual party had been rather dull, some sort of bar association get-together, but Melanie had been well-dressed and clearly respected by her peers.

Leann quirked an eyebrow and leaned closer. "How's the...you know...sex?"

That question was out of bounds. Easton didn't discuss his sex life with anyone, except maybe his brothers. He certainly didn't talk about it with his female cousin.

"That is none of your business," he replied crisply. "I can't believe you even asked me that."

Her mouth turned down and she shook her head again. "That bad, huh?"

The fact was he hadn't slept with Melanie. Not yet, anyway.

"My sex life is fine," he assured Leann. He didn't want to discuss this with her. "And since you're so fired up to discuss fornication, how's your sex life?"

He should have known she wouldn't shrink from answering. Leann had a spine of steel and with all the boys in the Anderson family she'd learned early not to back down from a challenge.

And he didn't need to know the details of her sex life with Zach.

Giggling, her eyes lit up and she grinned. "Fantastic, cousin. Absolutely awesome, thank you for asking." She poked her finger into the middle of his chest. "And that is the kind of sex life you should have. The kind that shakes the foundation of your house and wakes the neighbors. You need someone that excites you and gets you out of your rut. Someone that has more going on in their life than boring business. Someone…someone like Dizzy, for example."

Easton sputtered, almost spilling his drink. "Dizzy? The one and only Dizzy Foster? You must be joking. What in the hell would she and I talk about? Her latest aura cleansing? If you haven't noticed, Leann, your friend is weird. Bizarre. She passed up eccentric and is heading straight for crazy cat lady that all the kids in the neighborhood think is a witch."

Leann smiled sweetly. "Dizzy doesn't have a cat and she's not a witch. As for her aura…well, I cannot say but she's never mentioned that it was dirty."

With an image of Dizzy in his brain suddenly the word *dirty* took on a different connotation. He was going straight to hell for it too.

"She's still strange. Her name is Dizzy, after all."

Sighing, Leann refilled her wine glass. "That's because she couldn't pronounce *Desiree* when she was little. It came out sounding like Dizzy so it stuck. Don't be a jerk. Dizzy is a wonderful woman and you'd be lucky to date someone like her."

His cousin had lost her mind. Clearly being in love with Zach had moved around her brain cells until she couldn't think straight.

"I'm a man of logic and reasoning," Easton explained slightly exasperated. Leann wanted everyone to be in love. "Dizzy lights candles at the full moon and thinks crystals will cure her cold."

"It can't hurt," Leann shrugged. "It might even work. She never seems to be sick and she's happier than just about anyone I know. Maybe she's onto something and we should have a more open mind."

Easton had an open mind...but Dizzy was a bridge too far.

"No," he said firmly. "I don't think she and I would be good together."

His younger brother Carter took that opportunity to sidle up to them and horn in on the conversation. As usual. "Who wouldn't be good together?"

"Easton and Dizzy," Leann said with a smug smile. "Don't you think they'd make a great couple?"

Easton waited as Carter seemed to consider the pairing before answering. "It wouldn't be boring, that's for sure. Are you going to ask her out?"

Gritting his teeth together, Easton shook his head. "I am not. She's not my type. She's too...young for me."

He didn't even have the word for what Dizzy was. He only knew that she'd drive him crazy within minutes. She was sweet and lovely but mostly she was like a little sister to him. A strange little sister. That was not a recipe for romance and desire and passion.

Carter grabbed a beer from the cooler. "I doubt Dizzy would be interested in you anyway, big brother. You're a little too mainstream for her. She's probably looking for someone exciting and spontaneous."

Ouch, that kind of hurt. Easton knew that he wasn't spontaneous but he didn't need it pointed out to him. He liked to think of himself as calm and steady.

Although Carter and Leann would probably say that he was boring as hell.

Carter clapped a hand on Easton's shoulder. "I didn't come over here to debate the identity of your future wife with you. I came over here to tell you it's your turn with Madame Viola."

"Someone else can take my turn."

Chuckling, Carter took a swig of his beer. "That's what you say every single time."

At some point in the past, the party planner for the company had thought it would be funny and entertaining to hire a psychic for the event so she could tell everyone's "fortunes". While the staff appeared to really enjoy it, Easton thought it was ridiculous. But she was so popular they invited her back for almost every party. So far, he'd managed to avoid her.

"I'm saying it again. Leann, you can take my turn."

Tilting her head, his cousin looked him up and down for a moment. "I can but you know you're not helping the image of management? When you won't play along you make us look like we're not one of the team. That we're not all in this together and that you're too good or too important and busy to play along. Unless, of course, you do think that you're too important to spend five minutes with Madame Viola."

She had him and she knew it.

"Fine, let's get this over with. I have a lot of work to do."

With Carter on one side of him and Leann on the other, as if he might make a run for it, they walked across the room to where the psychic was holding court at a small table with several of the employees. They were all smiling and laughing as Easton approached, not looking forward to this at all. Viola would simply tell him a bunch of vague facts about himself that could be true for a multitude of people and then he could disappear back into his office.

Everyone would be happy. Not him, of course, but everyone else.

His other younger brother Shane stood up and motioned Easton toward the vacated chair across from Viola. "I hear it's your turn. Take my chair."

"Thanks," Easton mumbled. "Okay, let's do this."

He had no clue what a psychic was supposed to look like but Madame Viola took her appearance all the way. Short and round, she was dressed in purple and gold velvet with a plethora of jewelry on each hand and around her wrists and neck. Her dark hair, shot with gray, was piled on top of her head and secured with an ornate clip with multi-colored rhinestones. Even her shoes were over the top; high-heeled black boots with small gold buttons.

Giving him a smile, she reached for his hands with her plump fingers. Her skin was quite cool for the temperature of the room. "Now just relax and let me feel the energy around you. Do you have a specific question for me?"

How long will this last? Can I leave now?

"No."

"Then I'll just see where this takes us."

Hopefully it would lead him back to his office where he had

a bottle of aged scotch in the desk drawer.

Viola closed her eyes and seemed to sort of sway back and forth. For once the crowd around the table fell silent as they waited for her pronouncement like she was the Oracle of Delphi.

"You like control."

He was the CFO of a major corporation so that wasn't much of a deduction. He thought he heard Carter snort behind him but Easton stayed silent, waiting for this entire debacle to be over.

"You believe only in the physical world but the other realms haven't given up on you. They have plans that you won't be able to control."

More vague bullshit. This was becoming tiresome and he was losing patience.

"Your time of being alone is coming to an end. You'll need to make room in your life for a soulmate."

"You'll have to learn to put the toilet seat down," Carter laughed. "Leave work before midnight too."

Viola gave Easton's younger brother a pointed stare. "Do not disturb the reading, please."

"Sorry," Carter shrugged but was still smiling. "I couldn't resist. Please continue."

The psychic turned her attention back to Easton.

"Your soulmate is innocent....naive even....but she is surrounded by evil. She'll need you to be her champion."

Right. An innocent woman in today's society. So his soulmate was a virgin? He needed to get out of here before he said what he was really thinking.

"Okay, I need to be her champion. Anything else?"

Viola frowned and sighed heavily. "The road to love will be fraught with peril. It won't be easy. It might even be dangerous but it will be worth it."

More vague platitudes that could apply to half the people in the room. Easton gently tugged his hands from Viola's now tight grip.

"I'll keep all of that in mind. Thank you so much." With relief, he looked up at Leann. "Isn't your turn next?"

She nodded as her phone rang. "It is but just a minute. It's Dizzy."

"Maybe she heard us talking about her," Carter said with a chuckle. "Tell her I said hello."

Leann nodded again but her face had grown pale and her smile had disappeared. With every passing second as she listened, she seemed to grow more agitated.

"Just stay there," Leann commanded, her brow knitted together. "I'll be right over."

"What happened?" Easton asked as his cousin tucked away her phone and fumbled in her purse looking for her car keys. She appeared quite spooked and he didn't like to think of her driving. When she pulled the keychain from her purse he plucked it from her fingers before she could object.

"I think I should drive. You look like you're about to faint. What's going on? Is Dizzy okay?"

Leann's hand flew to her throat and her fingers visibly trembled.

"Dizzy witnessed a murder. I need to get to her right away."

Chapter Three

N O ONE BELIEVED Dizzy.

She'd told her story to the police that had shown up at her door only minutes after making the call but they hadn't bothered to hide their skepticism. It had only become worse when they'd practically battered down Trip's door and searched his house while she sat with a nice young cop in her living room, practically biting her nails down to the quick.

When the police had returned they'd informed her that there was no dead body in the house, no woman, no crime scene. Nothing out of the ordinary. They'd been rather smug about the whole situation as well as if she couldn't be trusted to know what was real and what wasn't.

Frantic at not being taken seriously, she'd called Leann who was now wading through the crowd of police in the living room, her cousin Easton trailing closely behind.

Great. Easton thinks I'm an idiot.

Leann threw her arms around Dizzy, giving her a reassuring hug. "What happened? Are you alright?"

Looking over Leann's shoulder, Dizzy could see Easton Anderson standing there with his hands on his hips, surveying the slightly chaotic scene unfolding around him. With his eyes narrowed and his lips pursed, he looked like he'd rather be anywhere but in her home.

He's welcome to leave.

Like all the Anderson men, he was handsome with his dark hair and crystal blue eyes but his personality kind of ruined it. He didn't mean to be impatient and short with her but somehow he always managed to no matter the situation, although he could be kind at times. Not long ago, he'd offered to give her a ride when it was raining. To his credit he'd never called her a freak out loud but she was sure he had in the deep, dark recesses of the computer he had for a brain.

"No one believes me," Dizzy replied to Leann's question, throwing up her hands in frustration. She wished now she'd never stepped foot outside this evening. "I saw Trip Stanford strangle a woman in the window but no one is taking me seriously."

Easton stepped forward, his brows pinched together. "That's a serious accusation, Dizzy."

Not only did he think she was weird, he also thought she was stupid as hell.

"I'm well aware of that," she said with as much patience and sweetness as she could muster. She'd had a particularly crappy evening and she wasn't going to take any shit from Easton Anderson. "Believe me when I say that I don't make this accusation lightly but I saw him do it. I was outside and I saw the whole thing."

More tears as the image of what had happened played again in her head, leaving her feeling overwhelmed by the situation.

She wasn't crazy. She'd seen it happen. It was like that movie *Gaslight* where someone was telling her that what she'd experienced really wasn't true. She couldn't trust her own senses, apparently.

Except that she wasn't wrong. And she knew it as well as she knew her own name.

Leann threw a nasty look over her shoulder at her cousin. "I believe you. Now start at the beginning and tell us what happened."

Amid all the officers milling around her home – they didn't seem to want to leave for some reason – Dizzy, Leann, and Easton found a quiet spot in the kitchen where she detailed her evening moment by moment until it had ended with a call to 911.

His arms crossed over his chest and still frowning, Easton didn't look convinced but he did seem willing to help. "Why don't I go talk to the officer in charge? See what he has to say."

That was a decent idea. The police weren't telling her much except that they hadn't found any evidence of what she'd reported. But Easton was a well-respected businessman in Tremont, plus his cousin West used to be the head of detectives before becoming mayor. If anyone could get them to talk, it would probably be him.

"Are you really okay?" Leann asked when Easton left them. "My God, it must have been horrible."

Both women shuddered but for different reasons. Leann at the thought of what she might have witnessed and Dizzy at the memories of what she'd involuntarily seen. The images would be burned in her brain for a long time to come. There was no way

19

she was sleeping tonight, or perhaps any night in the near future.

"It was but I'm glad that you're here." Dizzy rubbed at her eyes, still stinging from the tears she'd shed. "They don't believe me. They think I'm lying or that I'm crazy. I know that people in this town think I'm strange but I never imagined they'd think I was a liar."

People whispered behind Dizzy's back but she'd never felt it was mean-spirited. She'd always thought it was sort of amusing. Perhaps she had been too naive, too innocent.

"Everybody in Tremont adores you," Leann replied firmly. "They know all that you do for the community. Most people just think you march to your own drummer, that's all. No one thinks you're lying."

Dizzy nodded toward Easton who was speaking with one of the cops. "He does, and I think he has company."

"He doesn't. But you know how Easton is. It's all facts and numbers. If he can't experience something with his six senses he can't believe it. It doesn't have anything to do with you personally."

"Well, I saw this with my own eyes. I didn't make this up for fun or attention."

Easton and the officer approached Dizzy and Leann. The policeman shook Dizzy's hand. Funny how he hadn't wanted to discuss anything with her five minutes ago but a little chat from an Anderson male and he was all smiles.

"My name is Sergeant Baker and I'm the lead for this call, Miss Foster. We appreciate that you want to be a good neighbor and citizen of Tremont, please be assured of that. However, we haven't found any evidence of the crime that you claim you saw." The officer glanced at the table where her half-empty glass of wine sat. "Have you been drinking this evening, Miss Foster?"

"Now wait a minute," Leann protested loudly, her arm going around Dizzy protectively. "You cannot be serious? Dizzy is clearly not drunk."

Sergeant Baker straightened his shoulders as if ready to take a punch to the stomach. "I have to cover all the bases, ma'am. It's my job. Now Miss Foster, how much alcohol would you say you've had this evening?"

Dizzy didn't like the cop's line of questioning any more than her friend but she needed for these men to believe her so she was willing to answer. She didn't get a chance to, however, because Leann wasn't done.

"I had two glasses of wine at a party that I just left," Leann said, her lips pursed in distaste. "Don't you want to know about everyone's alcohol intake, Officer? You haven't asked my cousin yet. He was drinking whisky."

Easton stepped forward, his expression clearly not happy. "Can you give it a break, Leann?"

"No," she answered curtly. "They're trying to discredit our friend and I'm not going to stand for it."

Exhaling noisily, Easton turned to the policeman. "I have to agree with my cousin, Sergeant. Unless Dizzy was falling down drunk I don't see what difference it makes."

Not wanting to come between family, Dizzy held up her hand. "Thank you both but I have no issue answering that question. I drank half a glass of wine, maybe less before witness-ing...well...what I witnessed. I had a little more after I called 911 but as you can see I haven't finished the glass. That's it.

There's no great conspiracy here, Officer. I know what I saw and it was clear as day with the lights on in Trip's house. I saw him strangle that poor woman."

Sergeant Baker shuffled uneasily on his feet and nodded, making a note on a little pad of paper he'd pulled from a pocket. "Fine, you weren't impaired. Can you tell me how well you know Trip Stanford? Would you say that you two are...close?"

Dizzy had no idea where this cop was trying to go but she'd follow along for a few minutes and humor him.

"Not really. I met him when he moved to the neighborhood but we mostly just wave to one another. That's about it."

With raised brows, Baker scribbled something in his little notebook. "So you and Mr. Stanford weren't...romantically involved in any way?"

What in the...?

"No," she replied, her tone clipped. "Did he say that we were? Because I barely know him."

Leann was beside herself with anger, jumping up from her seat and even Easton was frowning now. Dizzy was also livid but had to keep her emotions under control. Already these men weren't inclined to believe her. If they thought she was a hysterical female she'd lose the little credibility she had.

A muscle ticked in Easton's jaw and she could see his hand reflexively go to his shirt pocket. There was the outline of a cell phone there. She had a feeling he was contemplating calling in reinforcements. Probably West. Or maybe Jason. "Sergeant, I'm not sure what any of that has to do with what Dizzy reported. She saw Trip Stanford strangle a woman. Have you investigated that at all?"

Baker cleared his throat and shifted on his feet again. "Of course we have, Mr. Anderson. Mr. Stanford invited us into his home and gave us full access. We found no one else in the home and Mr. Stanford says he was home all evening and had fallen asleep on the couch. There was no one there. No woman. No victim. So naturally I'm trying to get to the bottom of this claim."

Dizzy couldn't believe what she was hearing. "You didn't find her? You were barely over there for more than fifteen minutes. Where did you look? Did you check the attic? Or maybe a crawl space?"

Did she have to do everything for these policemen? Wasn't it enough that she'd witnessed the crime and reported it? Now she had to find the evidence too?

The officer cleared his throat. Again. Good, he was nervous. He should be.

"I can assure you that we searched the home thoroughly. There was no murder victim there, Miss Foster, which leads me back here to you."

Leann visibly bristled but Dizzy stood in front of her, ready to fight her own battles. "So I'm either drunk or looking for revenge for a love affair gone bad? It's like a lousy film noir, Sergeant. I can assure you that I am neither of those things. I saw a crime committed this evening and I reported it. Like a good citizen."

And no one seems to give a crap.

"Maybe you saw the television through the window," Baker suggested, a hopeful tone in his voice. "You could have mistaken it for live people."

Because I'm a nitwit?

"Except that I saw Trip with his hands around a woman's neck," she explained with far more patience than she was actually feeling. "I don't think he's starring in any movies or television shows."

The sergeant shoved his tablet into his pocket and sighed. "Listen, Miss Foster, there's nothing I can do here. You say you saw something but we can't find any evidence that anything happened in Mr. Stanford's home. You should be happy that he's been cooperative and doesn't seem to harbor you any ill will. He even said that you might have had woken from a bad dream and thought it was real. He's been quite nice through all of this."

She almost choked on her own spit. "Wait...I'm supposed to feel...sorry for him?"

The officer nodded. "You did falsely accuse him of murder, ma'am. Most neighbors wouldn't stand for that. I imagine he could sue you if he wanted to."

Easton growled and Leann didn't appear any happier.

"But I don't think he will," the cop added quickly. "As I said, he was extremely cooperative this evening."

Dizzy crossed her arms over her chest, her teeth snapping together. "Unlike me?"

Sergeant Baker spread his arms out as if to wash his hands of the entire situation. "You do have a reputation, Miss Foster."

Ouch. That hurt. A lot.

Her entire body shook with suppressed anger. They thought she was some kind of...kook.

"That's enough," Easton growled before she could reply. Her hands tightened into fists and her legs trembled. "I think it's time for you and your men to leave, Sergeant. Unless of course you have any more questions. We appear to have come to an impasse and the conversation is no longer productive."

As usual, Easton had summed things up perfectly. If she wasn't to be believed, she was done talking.

The sergeant wasn't done yet though. "If you want to change your statement, please give me a call. Really think about what you think you saw, Miss Foster, and then do the right thing."

So much for that whole protect and serve stuff.

"I won't be changing anything but thank you," she answered stonily.

Leann stayed with Dizzy as Easton herded the officers out of the house. Dizzy fell back into the chair and briefly covered her eyes with her hands as the sounds of their engines faded into the distance. They were gone and she was still here.

So was Trip Stanford. Just one door down. A murderer in her neighborhood. Usually the worst thing that happened around here was that someone didn't mow their lawn or they put a swarm of garden gnomes in the front yard.

Flipping the lock closed behind him, Easton came back to stand over them, his lips a grim line.

"That was a cluster," he said, his gaze flickering back and forth between his cousin Leann and Dizzy. "You need to figure out what happened here."

"I already know," Dizzy replied sharply. While she was grateful that Easton managed to get the police to speak to her, she wasn't inclined to take any guff from him either. "Trip strangled someone. Then apparently hid the body really well. But the cops don't believe me because I'm strange and a non-conformist to societal norms."

"They don't believe you because they didn't find a body," Easton argued, shaking his head. "If there had been a dead body over there it wouldn't have mattered who or what you were, Dizzy."

"*I have a reputation*," she mimicked. "Well, screw them and the horse they rode in on."

Shrugging, Easton lowered himself into a kitchen chair, his tone gentle. "C'mon Dizzy, you have to admit that you…you know. See things a little differently than others."

Anger and exhaustion were warring for dominance inside of her but a third emotion was actually winning the battle. Hurt.

"That's a crappy thing to say, Easton. Especially after what I've been through tonight. I saw someone murdered and you want to point out that I think Tarot cards might be real. You've known me practically my whole life but tonight I find out that you think I'm capable of lying."

A few tears slid down her cheeks and she huddled into herself on the chair, pulling her legs up and wrapping her arms around them so she could rest her chin on her knees.

Leann was no happier with Easton and she gave him a mean look, nudging him hard with the tip of her shoe. "You really were no help."

Easton rubbed his temple tiredly. "I defended Dizzy."

He had, but…

The words were out of Dizzy's mouth before she could stop them.

"Did you mean it, though? Or did you do it because of Leann?"

Stupid, stupid, stupid. Do not ask questions that you either already know the answers to or aren't going to like the replies that you get.

The pause before he answered was far too long. It said what he didn't want to say.

"I believe you think you saw something."

With Easton, it was probably the best she could ask for. But it begged the question: if someone who had known her for almost thirty years had doubts, how was she going to convince the police that she was telling the truth?

And what about Trip? He knew that she knew. Nothing good could come from that.

Chapter Four

I T WAS LIKE kicking a cute and tiny puppy.

Dizzy was a sweet woman. A little weird, but sweet. He wasn't sure what she'd witnessed tonight but she hadn't deserved that police officer's asinine questioning. She hadn't done anything wrong. She wasn't lovesick or drunk or whatever other excuse Baker had dreamed up. She truly believed she'd seen something. That much he knew was true. Everything else, however, was a mystery.

She was probably simply...confused. That was it. She was confused. She might have fallen asleep and woken, bleary-eyed from a dream and thought she saw something that had actually only been in her imagination. Of course she was going to call the police, and as quiet as Tremont was he doubted the cops had been busy with other major crimes. He'd bet whatever money was in his pocket that they'd been at the diner drinking coffee and eating apple pie. Tonight might be the most exciting thing that had happened to Officer Baker in months. Maybe years.

Leann had dug out three soda cans from the refrigerator and was currently pouring them into glasses, all the while slamming cabinets closed and just generally stomping loudly around the kitchen. Scowling, she shoved a glass at Easton after handing one to Dizzy, who accepted it with trembling hands.

"Thank you," he said, not wanting to argue with his cousin. Better to make nice if only for family harmony. "I can drive you home whenever you want to go."

Leann gave him an incredulous look. "For a man that graduated at the top of his class, you're not very smart. I can't leave Dizzy here with a murderer next door. Have you lost your mind?"

Easton didn't want to have to state the obvious. Trip Stanford wasn't a killer. The cops had proved that less than an hour ago.

"You don't have to stay," Dizzy protested. Her color looked much better than it had only minutes before. She'd always been a tough little kid. "I'll be fine."

Leann rolled her eyes and groaned. "I bet you don't even have a gun in this house to protect yourself."

Good guess. Tamara and Louis Foster had been lovely parents to Dizzy but a trifle on the hippie side. He couldn't see them teaching their daughter to shoot a gun as they were always vocal about hating violence. The Andersons hated violence too but everyone still learned how to handle a firearm by the time they were in their teens.

For the first time that evening, Dizzy smiled. "Actually, I do have one. I took lessons at the firing range to learn how to shoot it too. Don't tell Tami. She'll think I've turned to the Dark Side."

Another strange thing about Dizzy's mom and dad. She called them by their first names. They were more friends than parents, which was funny considering they had been older when they'd had her. All through Dizzy's childhood they'd encouraged their daughter to *express* herself. Don't conform. Consequently, their little daughter had taken some major shit from the kids in school when she put one foot outside the lines of what they considered normalcy. Through it all Dizzy acted as if she didn't care one iota. In fact, Easton couldn't remember one instance of complaining or crying on her part. Not one.

Not until tonight when they'd thought she was a liar.

"Your secret is safe with me but I'm still not leaving," Leann vowed. "You can't stay here alone. You're the only witness to a murder and that puts you in danger."

If there had actually been a murder, Easton would have wholeheartedly agreed. Except...there hadn't been and Leann was only feeding into whatever Dizzy had going here. A dream. A fantasy. A peyote vision. Whatever it was, Leann was encouraging it and she needed to stop. For Dizzy's sake.

Easton placed his hands on the kitchen counter. "Now let's think logically about this for a minute. Let's say that Trip Stanford did murder someone tonight. He knows that Dizzy called the police and that they've talked to her. If something happened to her, don't you think the first person they'd look at is Trip? He wouldn't want to call attention to himself. It would be crazy to go after Dizzy in any way. Better to keep her alive and not believed than to create more suspicion by hurting her."

"He'd make it look like an accident," Leann hissed, her face scrunched up.

"West and Jason are always saying that criminals aren't very bright," Easton shot back.

Dizzy hopped up from her chair and placed her glass next to the sink. "He was smart enough to kill a woman and hide her body so well that the cops couldn't find her. So he's not stupid." She sighed and rubbed at her temples. "I feel about a hundred years old right now. Everyone thinks I'm a gigantic liar but I know what I saw. Even if you don't believe me."

That last sentence was directed at him, of course. She was upset with him and in her shoes he wouldn't blame her. Except that the roles weren't reversed and he was apparently the only one in this house thinking clearly.

Scraping his fingers through his hair, he chose his words carefully. "I know you saw something here tonight. I'm just not sure that it was Trip Stanford strangling a woman."

Dizzy's brows shot up. "Please tell me what I might have mistook for a murder. A rousing game of Twister, perhaps?"

That did bring up an interesting theory.

"Maybe…they were…you know…"

Both women were looking at him like he was the dumbest person on the planet.

"I think he's speaking of sex," Dizzy said with a huff. "You can say it, you know. Nothing bad will happen if you say the word *sex* out loud. We're all adults here."

When the hell had that happened? Just yesterday he'd been helping Dizzy with her math homework and now she was a grown woman talking about sex. Crossing his arms across his chest, Easton kept his impatience under control. Leann and Dizzy were like little sisters to him and he didn't talk about sex with his little sisters. "Fine. Sex. Maybe they were having sex. Kinky sex."

Dizzy nodded as if she agreed. "Sure, that could be it. They were fooling around. *With the creepiest foreplay I've ever seen.*"

The last part was said loudly as she threw up her arms in disgust. She apparently didn't think much of his theory.

"I'm willing to entertain this little story." Leann sat down and crossed her legs, her body language belying her words. "If Trip Stanford was simply getting his freak on, why did he lie and say he was home alone and asleep all evening? Where was the woman?"

Easton shrugged. "These are all questions for West. I'm not a cop. Maybe she was married and didn't want to be found out. Maybe he was ashamed to be seen with her. I don't know. I'm just saying that there might be another explanation other than Dizzy lives next door to a killer."

A knock on the back door startled all three of them, interrupting any snarky reply the two women might have given. Dizzy opened the door and Easton couldn't believe his eyes at who stood there.

Trip Stanford. Just about the last person Easton expected to see. From Dizzy's wide eyes she hadn't expected it either. She'd taken several steps away from him which let Trip step into the kitchen.

The neighbor smiled weakly and shifted on his feet. "Um, hey. I just thought I should come over and tell you that there's no hard feelings, Dizzy. I mean that too. I'm sure you thought you saw something." He smiled more widely. "Maybe you saw a ghost or a spirit of some sort. The house is old, after all."

"A ghost?" Dizzy echoed dully. "You think I saw a ghost?"

This could get ugly fast. What had Stanford been thinking?

Tonight wasn't a good time to discuss this. Maybe tomorrow. Or the next day. Or ignore it and never speak of it. That's what Easton would have done. He was the king of ignoring something so it would go away. Ask any of his former girlfriends.

"It was probably just a nightmare," Trip replied, his gaze finally moving from Dizzy to Leann and then finally to Easton. "I'm Trip Stanford, by the way. I…uh…work for you. We've met a few times at the company Christmas party and the summer picnic."

The other man chuckled and Easton stepped forward to shake his hand, hoping Leann would do the same. It would be rude not to show some form of friendliness. The poor bastard wasn't having a good evening. Cops at his door. His house searched. He had to be wondering who he'd pissed off, karma-wise.

"Nice to meet you again. I think you're in the marketing department, right?"

Stanford grinned and nodded. "I am. Five years now. Very happy."

To his relief Leann had also moved closer, shaking Trip's hand and introducing herself. Because she'd been in Florida for so long, she hadn't yet met many of their employees.

"So…" Trip turned his attention back to Dizzy. "Seriously, it's okay. I just hope that you're fine because whatever sort of dream or nightmare you had must have been really scary and terrible. You might want to give up spicy food."

The neighbor had tried to make a joke but only Easton laughed a little. Dizzy and Leann were staying quiet. That was probably a good thing in the long run, although it was awkward as hell at the moment.

"I guess I'll go home." Trip stepped back onto the porch. "You all have a good evening."

Dizzy appeared to have woken up from whatever trance she'd been in. "Thank you for coming by, Trip. It was so…nice of you to let me know that you're not angry with me."

"Not mad at all," he assured her with a grin. "Now I'll say goodnight. See you at the office, Easton. Leann."

The younger man strode back to his house, entering through his own back door. Dizzy and Leann practically had their faces pressed against the windows watching him until he disappeared.

"Whew, that was creepy," Dizzy declared whirling around and shuddering visibly. "What the hell did he want, anyway?"

Leann was still staring out of the window, half-hidden by the daisy-covered curtains. "I don't know but he's up to no good. I think he was checking you out and maybe trying to find out what you saw or knew."

What in the hell?

Easton held up his hands. "Just stop this nonsense. He came over to say he wasn't pissed off. I think that was mighty nice of him. Not many people would do that, Leann."

Dizzy groaned and rolled her eyes. "*No one* would do that. *No one.* At least if they were innocent. They'd be angry and rightfully so to have been accused of murdering someone when they're innocent. And they sure as hell wouldn't get over that in less than an hour unless they were some sort of saint or heavily medicated. Only a guilty person would hurry over here and find out what was going on. I bet he's watching us right now. He wants to know what we're going to do."

Now it was Leann shuddering, rubbing her hands up and down her arms.

Easton had two women in front of him that had wild imaginations.

"He didn't ask anything about what you saw," Easton said. "He didn't try and get you to talk. He just came over to tell you that he's not mad. That's it. And he had to be pretty brave to do it too."

Dizzy elbowed Leann in the ribs. "Your cousin thinks we've blown this entire situation out of proportion. He thinks we're not being logical and that we need to be reasonable."

"I can't deny it," Easton growled. "That is true. Have you tried logic? It makes life so much easier."

He'd inadvertently lit a fuse and now both women were red in the face mad. At him.

"I didn't see a ghost." Dizzy stepped forward so they were toe to toe. The strawberry scent of her shampoo tickled his nostrils, incongruous with the little firebrand ready to kick his ass. Dizzy was a tiny thing, all big brown eyes and long chocolate-colored hair that she usually wore in a ponytail. "I didn't drink too much wine. I didn't fall asleep and have a nightmare. I didn't see Trip's television. I saw him strangle a woman with his bare hands. It might have been some kinky foreplay but she definitely fell to the floor when he was done. I. Saw. A. Murder. You may not like it when I say it but that doesn't make it any less true, Easton. I only wish you'd witnessed it too because I know that's the only way you'd believe me. It's just the way you are. You can't help yourself."

This entire night had gone into the toilet and it had all started at that stupid party with the psychic. Now it was ending in Dizzy's kitchen. She was a good person, giving and sweet, but he couldn't allow her to continue entertaining this fantasy. It did no one any good to humor her.

"I wish I had too," he finally said. "Try to get some sleep tonight and maybe things will look different in the morning."

The corners of Dizzy's lips turned up. "You mean maybe I'll have come to my senses. That I'll become…logical. More like you. That's not going to happen. I saw a woman being murdered tonight. That's not something that's just going to go away after a few hours' sleep. I need to figure out what I'm going to do about it. What the next step is."

Oh hell no. He needed to nip this in the bud right now.

"There is no next step," he said firmly. "You're not going to do a goddamn thing. Leave this alone, Dizzy. Leave Trip Stanford alone too or he will sue you. Or call the police on you for harassment. Just leave it all alone."

Dizzy and Leann exchanged a glance that Easton didn't like. They'd always get into mischief whenever they were together. Dizzy was a bad influence on Leann. Or vice versa.

"Please say that you'll leave it alone," he pleaded. "Promise me."

"I'll do nothing of the kind," Dizzy replied crisply. "Frankly, you're beginning to piss me off, Easton Anderson. You're pretending to be on my side but you're just like Officer Baker and all his men. You think I'm weird and a liar. Now you can leave my house. I've had quite enough of people telling me what I did and didn't see for one night."

The tiny tornado of a woman strode over to the front door

and opened it. She just stood there waiting for him to move, her toe tapping on the maple flooring.

"So you're staying then?" he asked Leann, palming his car keys in his pocket. He was ready to leave. Dizzy might be tired of him but he was exhausted from her. Heaven help the man she ended up with. She'd have him chasing his tail on a daily basis. The poor asshole would have to lock himself in a closet to get a moment's peace.

"I am."

He walked to the door where he paused in front of Dizzy. He hadn't wanted to hurt her but he clearly had. Good intentions and all that. But he also couldn't believe her wild story when the police had found no evidence that it had happened.

Real physical evidence. She had zero. How could she expect him – or anyone else – to believe her?

"I am sorry," he said before he left. "As I said earlier, I believe that you believe something happened."

She looked up at him, her normally soft brown eyes dark with hurt. He'd hurt her and he'd try and find a way to make it up to her. Somehow.

"It's no big deal. As I said before, you can't help yourself." Dizzy shrugged but he could see her lips tremble with emotion. His chest tightened uncomfortably at how vulnerable and sad she looked. As if she needed to be protected from life, except that was nonsense. Dizzy had been taking care of herself for years. Just fine too.

Your soulmate is innocent....naive even....but she is surrounded by evil. She'll need you to be her champion.

To his chagrin, the words of the psychic earlier in the evening came rushing back. But Dizzy wasn't his soulmate. Heck, they barely spoke to one another when they were in the same room. If she was the one, he would have known long ago. Right?

"I have to go," he said, his fingers tightening on his keys. "Call me if you need me."

Leann waved him away. "We won't. Now go."

Having officially worn out his welcome, he jumped into his vehicle and pulled out of the drive, heading straight for home. He needed a whiskey and a comfortable bed after the day and night he'd had. If Leann wanted to indulge Dizzy's fantasies then she was welcome to. He wasn't going to do it. Someone had to be the rational one around here, and lately that job had fallen to him.

Chapter Five

DIZZY YAWNED AND shifted on the couch before taking another fortifying sip of coffee. She didn't want to fall asleep. Not with a killer living so close.

"Park Place," Leann announced with triumph. "You owe me fifty bucks."

Both women had changed into pajamas – Leann borrowing a pair of Dizzy's – and they'd hunkered down for the night, determined to keep watch on the home next door in case Trip decided to move the body away from the house. To that end, they'd set up a *Monopoly* game between them on the sofa where they could see the street from a gap in the drapes. If anyone left their home tonight, they'd see it.

"Here you go." Dizzy handed over the money with less than enthusiasm. Her mind was only partially on the game and it showed. She was getting thoroughly trounced, although *Monopoly* wasn't her preferred game. She was better at *Clue* but they'd both thought that a game based on a murder wasn't a good choice. "It's so quiet this time of night. Kind of creepy, isn't it?"

Leann pushed the dice closer to Dizzy. "I think that what happened tonight makes it creepy, not the silence. Can you see anything?"

"Nothing. Not even a cat. Wouldn't he want the body out of the house? I mean…unless he's doing something awful with it." Dizzy shuddered again. "Now I'm freaking myself out."

Twisting her body around, Leann peeked out of the curtains for a moment. "I have a theory. After Trip strangled that girl, he probably panicked. I know I would. So then what would he do?"

"Dispose of the body," Dizzy replied immediately. "That's what I'd do, especially if people knew she was with me."

"But if they didn't know," Leann countered. "And you were scared, you might stuff the body away and then try and calm down. You know, think about what you should do and where you would get rid of the body and the evidence. But I guess that's the opposite of panicking. So if he didn't panic, this might not be his first murder."

Placing her hand on her now nauseous stomach, Dizzy gulped down the acid that had gathered in her mouth. "That's just lovely. I live on Serial Killer Boulevard. This is going to hit home values hard."

Leann turned to check the street again. "You're going to have to move now. You know that, right? You can't stay here."

That very thought had crossed Dizzy's mind more than once this evening.

"If they don't end up arresting him," she pointed out. "Eventually he's going to have to get rid of the body and we'll be here watching him. Do you think he knows that he's being watched? Is he watching us watching him?"

This was worse than when she'd watched a double feature of *Terror Train* and *Prom Night*. All alone. She'd quickly learned what a nightmare really was like.

Leann pursed her lips in thought for a long moment before answering. "Honestly? No. I think the arrogant little prick thinks he got away with it. The way he came over here tonight so confident and smug. He thinks that no one is going to believe you no matter what you say and that he can charm you into thinking you had a bad dream or something. Did you see how he was laying it on thick with Easton? How he loved his job and all that crap but the whole time he was watching you."

"And now we're watching him. And I bet he knows that we are. He's not going to do anything with that body tonight, is he? He's going to wait a day or two until he thinks we've lost interest or believe his story."

Leann stood and padded into the kitchen, retrieving the coffee carafe to refill their mugs.

"I know this is going to sound macabre but where do you think he hid her?"

Dizzy rubbed her pounding temple. She'd had a headache for hours and it showed no signs of waning any time soon. "You're only saying out loud what I've been thinking silently. These houses on this cul de sac and down the street are almost identical in layout. If it were me I might stow her in a corner of the basement or perhaps in the crawlspace behind the powder room. I think there's enough room and the opening isn't conspicuous at all. Anyone could walk right by it and not even know it's there."

Leann's brows were pinched together as she poured the coffee. "You have a crawl space behind the bathroom? Where? I've never seen it and I helped you move in to this house. I lived here with you for months."

"Follow me. I'll show you."

Dizzy led the way down the hall toward the laundry room. The half bath was next to it and then there was a small alcove that led to the garage. She pointed to the white-washed wainscoting on the wall.

"Right there."

Leann bent down closer, but she shook her head. "I don't see— Wait, there it is. Just a gap in the wainscoting, barely enough to get your fingers in there. You wouldn't know unless you were looking for it. Holy hell, you could really hide something or someone back here."

Swinging the small door open, Dizzy knelt down to look inside the dark space. She didn't use this for anything as she hated any and all creepy crawlers. If she'd opened her Christmas decorations and found a spider the holidays would definitely be cancelled that year.

But there was room for a dead body. Not much more but a determined person could make it work.

"For awhile," Dizzy replied, although her mind was already working on just how long that was a feasible choice for Trip. Eventually... "But he can't leave her there for long. He needs a more permanent solution. Jeez, listen to the way we're talking about it. So cold-blooded and clinical."

Leann nodded sagely. "Your more rational mind is taking over for the emotional part of your brain until you process all your feelings about what you witnessed tonight. Classic reaction and nothing to worry about. You're normal."

As a licensed psychologist, Leann's opinion could be trusted.

"Your cousin doesn't think that. He thinks I'm a liar and a weirdo."

It still stung that Easton hadn't believed her. She shouldn't have expected it but there was a small part of her that had hoped he would. She should probably just be grateful that he had intervened with the police and leave it at that.

Leann levered off the floor and helped Dizzy close up the crawlspace. "Easton needs a good smack every now and then. I apologize for his crappy attitude tonight but you know how he is. A computer for a brain and a cash register for a heart. I pity the woman he eventually marries."

They turned out the lights behind them as they headed back into the living room, hoping they hadn't missed anything happening on the street. Dizzy took up her position on the couch again.

"I don't know about that. Easton is the type that once he falls in love he'd be a dedicated husband. He'd never cheat on her."

Leann snorted. "That's true. He'd never want to admit that he was that human. As for falling in love, I can't even imagine how he would do that. He makes everything about profit and loss, pros and cons. I heard him tell Jason once that he should select his wife carefully because she had to fit into the Anderson family. Can you believe that? Like I would have launched Zach if he didn't get along with my brothers and cousins? I highly doubt he's ever been in love. Not really."

Frankly Dizzy couldn't imagine Easton in love either, although until this moment she hadn't given it any thought. He had many wonderful qualities but he had a few others that made her crazy. Not that it mattered. She wasn't interested in Easton Anderson. He might be handsome as hell but he was a pain in the ass.

"Do you think you could call Zach?" Dizzy suggested meekly. Leann's fiancé was currently out of town for work. "Not now obviously but maybe tomorrow? Maybe he could…you know…check out Trip Stanford. He's lived in Tremont a long time but what does anyone know about him?"

She hated suggesting it but the police weren't going to lift a finger to help her. If she wanted anything done she was going to have to call in a few favors.

Leann slapped down her coffee mug. "That's a great idea. Why didn't I think of that? Zach can do a little background check on your neighbor. Who knows what he was up to before he moved here? I'll call him in the morning, first thing. Which is in approximately four hours."

Checking the deserted street one more time, Dizzy stood and headed to the kitchen.

"I better put on another pot of coffee then. Is it my turn or yours?"

It was going to be a long night and no way was Dizzy going to shut her eyes for even one minute of it.

Chapter Six

AS A MEMBER of the Anderson family, Easton took his responsibilities to the town of Tremont quite seriously. That was why he had volunteered to be a judge in the Anderson Industries sponsored art contest being held at the community center. That explained why he was standing in the middle of a crowd with his younger brother Carter looking at a row of paintings from some of Tremont's most artistic citizens. And more than a few who didn't have a creative bone in their body but they enjoyed taking the classes and socializing.

When he'd remembered where he needed to be this morning he'd almost called in sick but his innate sense of honesty simply wouldn't let him do that. He was going to have to tough out the day but it wasn't going to be easy, because the one person he didn't want to see was in charge of the art contest.

Dizzy. Looking especially lovely today dressed in a black sleeveless dress covered with brightly colored flowers. The skirt was short enough that it showed off her tanned and toned thighs.

Why am I looking at her legs? Stop it right now. What's happening to me?

It was all that talk last night at the party about how Dizzy would be the perfect woman for him. That the other females he dated were boring and she was spontaneous and unpredictable. Now he was noticing her in ways he hadn't before and he didn't like it one little bit. It was wrong.

Dizzy might be pretty and eccentric but she selflessly gave her time to teach painting and sculpting at the center. Which was how he'd been roped into this job in the first place. She'd attended one of the famous Anderson Sunday dinners and had corralled himself and Carter in the kitchen appealing to their civic duty and not letting them out until they'd agreed. So here he was and it was awkward as hell. Just a few hours ago she'd ordered him out of her house.

For good reason, too.

After the few hours of sleep he'd managed to grab he'd come to the conclusion that although he was right about Trip Stanford not being a killer, that didn't mean that Dizzy didn't totally believe she'd seen a murder. He could have been more under-standing and saved the tough love for the light of day. She had to have been terrified in her own home last night and that didn't sit well with him at all.

He wasn't the kind of man to leave a woman in distress on her own. At least he hadn't thought that he was but his behavior said something different. Sure, Leann had been there and she could kick some major ass, but he hadn't been the gentleman he'd thought he was. Her situation had been *inconvenient* and incompatible with his busy schedule so he'd acted like an ass. His only saving grace was that he truly didn't believe Dizzy was in any danger at all.

"What do you think?"

Carter's voice penetrated Easton's distant thoughts as he stared sightlessly at an abstract multi-colored painting with huge splashes of red. He had no fucking idea what this was supposed to represent and it looked like a finger-painting from a toddler. This was art?

"It's very…red."

His brother must have thought Easton's reply was hilarious because he cracked up, hiding his face behind his arm and pretending to write something down on his clipboard.

Carter pointed to the card next to the painting. "It's supposed to represent a woman's struggle against a patriarchal society."

Easton sympathized with the female's frustration regarding asshole chauvinists but that didn't help him understand the painting.

"It's red," he repeated, raising his brows at the explanation. It sounded like a bunch of crap. "It might go well in Leann's house. She likes red."

"You do not buy art to match your throw pillows, Easton." That voice. He'd been avoiding her all day, dealing with her assistant, but he was caught now. "You buy it because it speaks to your heart and soul. Because it evokes a strong emotion inside of you. It would appear that this piece doesn't move you in any way."

Slowly turning around, Easton steeled himself against what would surely be one pissed off female but this one wasn't giving him the stink eye as he'd expected. Her pretty features were serene and composed as if it was someone else who had ordered him out of her house last night. Someone that looked just like her.

"I wouldn't say it doesn't evoke any emotion at all," Easton heard himself say. "It's just not a strong one."

Dizzy nodded as if he was making sense. "People all react to art differently. You might have more luck outside of the abstract realm."

His younger brother placed his hand on Dizzy's shoulder and Easton had the strangest urge to knock it away. There was no reason for Carter to be touchy-feely with Dizzy. They weren't all that close, at least as far as he was aware.

"How are you?" Carter asked, his trademark grin wiped from his face and a more sober expression taking its place. "Are you hanging in there?"

Leann must have called Carter or maybe she'd talked to Noah, who had talked to Carter. Either way, the news was out.

Dizzy's own smile had disappeared as well but she nodded bravely, her shoulders straightening. "I'm okay. Shaken up but okay, although I will say that Leann and I didn't get a wink of sleep last night."

"I would imagine not. What are you going to do now?"

Nothing.

"Leann talked to Zach this morning and he's going to check out Trip Stanford. See if there's anything from before he came to Tremont." She lowered her voice even more, barely a whisper. "I'm also going to keep an eye on the house. He might try and move the body soon."

There was no body. No murder. He felt badly about his behavior last night but Dizzy's belief in what she'd seen hadn't diminished in the least. If anything, she looked more determined than ever.

Shit. This was not good.

"Zach's a good guy and if anything is there he'll find it." Carter nodded approvingly. Did his brother actually believe what Dizzy was saying? The entire Anderson family had lost their minds. "Let me know if you need any help. I'd take a shift watching for some of your famous snickerdoodles."

Dizzy was smiling again. "That sounds like a great deal. I might even throw in some apple pie too."

Dizzy's cooking was legendary in about three counties. Maybe more.

"Now wait a minute," Easton heard himself objecting. "Apple pie is my favorite. Carter likes cherry."

"I like apple," Carter contradicted with a laugh, reaching out to touch her arm. Again. "I like everything Dizzy cooks. Seriously, call me if you need anything at all."

Well, aren't you the helpful one?

Carter was flirting with Dizzy. *Flirting.* The last thing Dizzy needed was a horn dog like Easton's brother chasing her around with his tongue hanging out. She deserved better than that.

"We should get back to work," Easton said, clearing his throat to get their attention. "We have a lot to do and people are waiting for the results."

Narrowing his eyes, Carter gave him an appraising look. "Sure, we probably should get back to the business at hand." He waved toward the painting. "I guess I don't really understand how to figure out what it's trying to say and how we're supposed to judge it."

She smiled then, her pink lips turning up at the corners, showing off dimples in her cheeks. He'd noticed them before, of course, but somehow today they looked different. But that wasn't really possible. Unless maybe this really wasn't the same Dizzy from last night.

Great. Now she's got me believing in that paranormal bullshit.

"You don't have to understand it. Your cognitive response isn't important here, your emotional one is." She motioned toward the painting. "The red represents the artist's anger at society around her, which has grown larger than the other feelings represented by the different colors. Green for serenity, yellow for happiness, blue for sadness, and so on. But you don't need to know that to judge it. You only need to tap deep down into your heart and decide how it makes you feel, even if the only thought you have is that it's pretty or ugly."

Dizzy had gone to art school so this all came naturally to her. Easton? This was like learning a foreign language when you had to go to the bathroom really badly but didn't know the right words to be able to ask someone where it was located.

"I think I may be the wrong person for this job," Easton said, frowning at the rows of paintings on the walls of the center. "You should have asked Leann. She's all about feelings."

Carter scratched on his clipboard. "I think we can handle this. I know what I like and don't like."

"Perfect. I really do appreciate you both helping out today. And I do have Leann helping out as well. She's judging the sculpture entries in about an hour."

A small group of people had wandered close by to look at the artwork. Two couples who were clearly old enough to know better were giving Dizzy sly looks and not bothering to hide their laughter.

The news about her call to the police had obviously gone viral all over Tremont. Nothing was faster or more efficient than the gossip in a small town. Twitter had nothing on Tremont's rumor mill.

Easton scowled at the people but Dizzy laid a hand on his arm and shook her head. "Don't bother. It's been happening to me all day. I found a drawing of a ghost on the door this morning when I opened up. If you give them any attention it will only encourage the behavior."

"It's bullshit," he growled, practically baring his teeth to the two couples who quickly vacated the area, almost falling over each other in their haste. Good. They'd known what they were doing was wrong but they all knew that Dizzy was too sweet to say anything. But Easton wasn't. "You don't have to take this."

Dizzy looked him right in the eye, her own expression hard. "You didn't have any problem dishing it out last night, so I think you might want to check your hypocrisy meter. It's in the red. Now, where were we? Right, you were judging these paintings. Do you have any more questions? If not, I need to check in with the other judges."

She didn't wait for his answer, whirling around and striding away. His gaze landed on the sway of her hips for a second too long because Carter was now grinning like an idiot.

"Clearly there is more going on between you two than this art contest. Care to share, big brother? This has to be a great story."

"It's not," Easton replied bluntly. "Dizzy and I had a few

words last night. End of story. See? Not so fascinating."

"Are you sure? Because the tension between you two is almost electric and a hell of a lot more than a tiff."

Easton shrugged, not willing to go into the details with his brother. "Just a disagreement. She wasn't happy that I didn't believe her about Stanford. We had words about it and she asked me to leave."

Carter's brows shot up to his hairline. "You don't believe her? You think she's lying?"

There was incredulity in Carter's tone but he simply didn't understand.

"Of course, I don't think she was lying. I believe that she thinks she saw something. But there is no evidence that there was any murder, so clearly, she didn't see what she thinks she did. But yes, I believe she believes it."

Carter glanced over to where Dizzy was speaking animatedly to a few of her students. "But she's a little crazy so she can't have actually witnessed what she said she did? Right?"

Carter actually sounded like...

"You believe her?"

"Sure do."

This day was becoming as strange as last night. Cue the *Twilight Zone* music.

"Even though there's no evidence at all?"

"Yep, because Dizzy wouldn't lie."

Everyone kept thinking Easton thought she was lying. He didn't think that.

"I didn't say she–"

Carter held his hand up. "I don't want to hear your lame excuses. You're always saying how weird Dizzy is but she's really not. And she's absolutely not the type to make something like this up. If she says she saw something then she saw something. That's it."

Easton stepped closer so they wouldn't be overheard. "You think Trip Stanford is a killer?"

"I don't know if he killed anyone but I sure as hell know that Dizzy saw him in an altercation with someone." Carter frowned as if he couldn't figure out Easton. "We've known her practically our entire life. When has she ever made an accusation like this? I don't know what happened last night but I know that something bad happened. You might want to try being a little more supportive. She's been through hell and here she is walking and talking like normal today. Not many could do that."

That was true. Even if the murder didn't happen, Dizzy was convinced it had and that had to be traumatic.

Wait a minute. If the murder didn't happen?

He was losing his mind too.

"I should probably apologize."

Carter wrote on his clipboard and then moved down to the next painting. "You think?"

Easton owed her an apology. A good one. Groveling wasn't his favorite thing to do but he'd do it. Dizzy was a nice person and she deserved it.

"She said that I couldn't help myself. That it's in my nature to want physical evidence," he said defensively. If she understood did he still have to apologize?

"That's true. Doesn't make it any better though. You need to say you're sorry or Mom is going to chew you a new asshole if she finds out how you acted."

None of the Anderson boys ever wanted to piss off their mother. She never yelled but she had a way of being disappointed that had much more of an effect. Now their father? He yelled. And then sent them out to do the worst chores on the ranch as a punishment.

"How would she find out? Do you think Leann will tell her?"

He knew Dizzy wouldn't. She wasn't a tattletale. Never had been.

That cocky grin was back on Carter's face. "If she doesn't, I will. Now let's get this done so you can go grovel a little."

Something Easton wasn't very good at.

Chapter Seven

DIZZY HANDED A scoring sheet to Leann as the sculpture portion of the judging began. Easton and Carter were done with the paintings and had retreated to the far side of the community center for punch and cookies, much to Dizzy's relief. She was vacillating between wanting to thank Easton for trying to defend her and punch him in the nose for being a butthead. Neither of those emotions were conducive to running an art show and contest so it was better if she didn't speak to him the rest of the day.

"Just remember to have fun with this," Dizzy reminded her friend. "Don't try and analyze things too deeply. Think with your heart."

Leann nodded and clipped the score card to the clipboard she'd been given. "Let me guess. Cousin Easton tried to find some magic mathematical formula he could use to judge the paintings? He's a financial genius but I worry about him sometimes."

Raising a brow, Dizzy glanced over toward the door where Easton was having an animated conversation with one of Dizzy's art students, a lovely retired lady named Annabelle Dalton who liked to paint nudes, specifically her husband. If she wasn't mistaken, Annabelle was doing a little flirting. Dizzy couldn't really blame the woman; after all, Easton Anderson was handsome with his short, dark hair, piercing blue eyes, and muscled physique that belied his desk job. She knew for a fact that all of the Anderson boys made a point to work on the ranch from time to time but Easton also belonged to the same gym as Dizzy.

He just went way more than she did.

"He seems like he has his life well in hand," she observed. "Why would you worry?"

"He's all alone."

It looked like from choice because no Anderson man ever had to be by himself unless he wanted it that way. Way too many women in about five counties were hoping to land one of the few single ones left.

"So were you not long ago," Dizzy pointed out. "Maybe he's happy."

"Maybe." Leann shrugged. "Now before I start the judging I want to tell you what Zach said. He called me this morning and we had a long talk."

Wrinkling her nose, Dizzy looked over her shoulder again to where Easton was now talking to his brother Carter, having shaken Annabelle. "Does he think I'm as crazy as Easton does?"

"Not in the least. He thinks you need to be careful. Very careful. He's going to check out Trip Stanford's background but in the meantime, I'm moving in with you. Unless, of course, I can convince you to leave your house and move in with me. You'd be safer."

"I can't leave," Dizzy protested. "I have to keep an eye on

him."

"I told Zach that's what you'd say," Leann sighed. "Then I'm staying with you. And you know what that means... Sunday dinner at the Andersons. I think it's roast chicken this week."

Dizzy didn't want her friend to disrupt her entire life because of this but she had to honestly admit that she'd feel better if she had company. Her home, which had been a haven less than twenty-four hours ago, was now creepy as hell.

"You don't have to stay with me."

She didn't sound convincing and Leann just laughed. "We can have fun. Like when I was living with you. It'll be great."

It would only be for a few days. Zach would be home on Tuesday and surely Leann wouldn't stay then.

"Fine, and thank you. It is a little unsettling."

A major understatement but Dizzy wasn't a woman who would allow herself to crawl away to relive those horrifying moments over and over. She'd already decided that she had to be strong. Few people were taking what she said seriously so she was going to have to prove she was telling the truth all on her own.

She'd witnessed a murder and somehow she would prove it.

EASTON DIDN'T KNOW what the hell was wrong with him but he was beginning to think that he might be having some sort of early mid-life crisis. Here he was having a nice dinner with his sort of girlfriend Melanie Elliott and he was thinking about little Dizzy Foster. He should have his head examined.

Melanie was a local real estate attorney, educated and successful. She could pair wine with any meal and could talk about books, opera, and current events, although she was intelligent enough to shy away from topics too controversial that might ruin the digestion over dinner. She was also quite lovely, with her honey blonde hair styled conservatively into what he'd heard described as a "bob" that just brushed her chin. Her hair wasn't long and wild like Dizzy's and she didn't wear bright lipstick, preferring soft tones that didn't draw too much attention.

All in all, Melanie was perfect for Easton. She'd make an excellent wife and an asset to the Anderson family. She'd easily fit into his life whether he had to attend a cocktail party in New York or a lavish sit-down dinner in London. She'd know what fork to use and how to charm the stranger sitting next to her at the table.

And he was utterly and completely bored to death.

If there was one true thing he could say about Dizzy it was that he was never, ever under any circumstances bored when he was with her.

Frustrated? Amused? Puzzled? Yes, all of those things. But never bored.

This was Leann's fault. She'd brought it up and now he couldn't get it out of his head. Carter too had to take some blame. They'd said that he dated boring, unexciting women. They'd even suggested that he date Dizzy. Now here he was, comparing his perfectly wonderful girlfriend to a woman that was more like a little sister. And the girlfriend was coming out on the short end. What the hell had happened to him? Clearly, he'd had a blow to the head that he didn't remember. Which would make sense if he had some type of short-term memory loss but then wouldn't his head be sore?

Melanie sipped her pinot noir. "So the negotiations are going to continue but I know we'll win out in the end. They don't have much leverage."

About what? He had to admit that he'd stopped listening a while ago. She'd been telling him about some deal she was negotiating on behalf of an out of town buyer. He wanted to purchase a large parcel of land and build townhouses. Melanie had already recommended Anderson Construction for the job and Easton should be thrilled. It would mean more housing choices in the Tremont area, plus a bountiful new contract for Anderson Industries.

Except that he couldn't help but think that Dizzy wouldn't like it. She'd say that the housing wasn't that affordable and urban sprawl was an ugly thing. She wouldn't be all that thrilled about what they'd have to do to all that unspoiled land either. Maybe Easton could convince the buyer to set aside some of the acreage and build a park. It might engender some local goodwill.

"Easton, you've barely spoken this evening."

Pulled from his reverie, he couldn't disagree. He'd been quiet and brooding tonight and none of that was Melanie's fault.

"I'm sorry. I guess I have a lot on my mind tonight."

Her brows pinched together sympathetically. "Work? Why don't you tell me about it?"

He usually did. He and Melanie had somehow managed to steer clear of more personal topics in the six or so dates they'd had together. He really didn't know much about her, to be truthful. Maybe there was much more to her than real estate law.

"Tell me something about yourself. Something I don't know."

The words just came tumbling out of him and he'd been powerless to stop them. This was why he liked control. No surprises.

"Something about myself?" Her head tilted and she appraised him as if trying to figure out what alien entity had taken over his body. "Why don't you start?"

A reasonable request.

Except that he didn't like to talk about himself. It made him uncomfortable to reveal intimate details of his life. But he'd asked her so…

"I once thought I wanted to be a doctor," he replied. "But I eventually changed my mind and went into finance."

"Why did you change your mind?"

This was a subject he hadn't thought about in years so he had to think for a minute as to why he had. It seemed like a lifetime ago.

"I wanted to work in the family business."

Melanie smiled and took a sip of her wine. "If you'd become a doctor I bet Tremont would have the best hospital in the United States with a wing named after your family."

He shrugged. "It wasn't meant to be. I think I found a vocation that I have a passion for."

"True." Melanie played with the stem of her glass. "I guess it's my turn. Let's see, something about myself that you don't know. How about…I was engaged once to my high school sweetheart."

"Obviously you called it off."

"We went to different universities. Long distance proved insurmountable. So is that what you were looking for?"

Was it? He didn't feel any closer to Melanie. The fact was he liked her and she was lovely but if this was really going to work he probably shouldn't be sitting here comparing her to Dizzy. That action didn't bode well for their relationship.

"It was," he began cautiously. Breaking Melanie's heart was horrid but he had to be truthful. "It's just that—"

"This isn't working between us," she finished for him, her smile growing wider.

She didn't look upset in the least. If anything, she looked happy. And relieved. Damn.

"I don't think it is," he conceded, blowing out a breath. "I'm really sorry."

"There isn't any chemistry. I wanted to be attracted to you but something is missing."

All this honesty was hell on his ego.

Frowning, Melanie reached across the table and grabbed his hand. "That didn't come out quite the way I'd planned it. What I meant to say is that you're a handsome man but I don't think you're all that attracted to me either, are you?"

No, but he was too much of a gentleman to say so.

"You're a beautiful woman, Melanie."

Apparently, that was funny because she began to laugh. "Well, thank you but I still don't think you're attracted to me. Not in…that way."

The entire situation was awkward and it underlined to him why he avoided personal conversations. They were uncomfortable as hell.

"I just don't think I'm the man for you, Melanie. You deserve better than a workaholic. I just don't have the time to devote myself to a relationship right now."

"There's no heat between us." Melanie smiled knowingly. "No passion, no chemistry. When you find the right one, you won't care so much about dollars and cents."

She sounded like a woman who knew all about that. Which could only mean one thing.

"You've already met someone else, haven't you?" he sighed, taking a gulp of his own wine. His heart wasn't hurt but his ego was slightly banged up. "Why did you accept my dinner invitation?"

"Because I wanted to tell you in person," she said softly. "But you made it much easier for me, so thank you. We've both been fooling ourselves these last weeks, thinking there might be something there between us. Clearly, we were meant to be just friends, and I hope we can stay that way."

"We can."

Of course, they could. Easton was nothing if not a rational man who didn't let emotion sway his day to day decision making.

Jesus, he sounded boring as shit. No wonder Melanie had found someone else. He'd become an old fart at forty-one.

But he had no earthly idea how to change that. Or if he even wanted to.

Leann and Dizzy. They were making him crazy and now he was questioning his life choices. He was going to banish both of them from his brain cells. There was nothing wrong with the way he lived his life. Not one thing. He wasn't boring either. Although he was now alone. Again. Another burgeoning relationship nipped in the bud. Perhaps he was meant to live his life this way.

It wouldn't be so bad. He would control the thermostat and the remote. He'd never have to watch a chick flick and he didn't have to rinse his whiskers out of the sink. He could leave the seat up to his heart's content and eat Chinese takeout at three in the morning.

If he dated a woman like Dizzy he'd be going to psychic readings and helping her rearrange her healing crystals. He might even have to take up yoga.

Better to be alone than to do a Downward Facing Dog. A man had to have some dignity in this world.

✦　　✦　　✦

LATER THAT EVENING, too restless to sleep, Easton had gone for a run, hoping that exercise would wear out his body enough that he could quiet his mind. His brain simply wouldn't turn off for even thirty seconds, darting from one thought to another until it felt like his head might explode.

Running through the streets of Tremont, his feet pounded the pavement as he breathed in the cooler night air, heavy with the perfume of freshly cut grass and flowers. Somewhere off in the distance a dog barked when he passed their house but he didn't break stride, determined to return home completely exhausted. His thoughts, however, refused to cooperate, sifting through his mind as he tried to make some sense of the last few days.

He wasn't too sure that he was happy with who he'd become. A grumpy workaholic who relied on profit and loss statements to fill his evenings instead of human companionship.

It had been fine for awhile, but after tonight with Melanie his cold, empty future yawned in front of him. He wasn't a man who believed in being lonely; after all he had a huge family and lots of friends. But there were times when he saw his brothers and cousins all marrying and starting families he wondered if there was someone out there for him. Then the thought would drift out of his mind, replaced with the more mundane details of his life but now they were lingering more often and longer.

Was this all there was to life? To his life in particular?

He was at the top of his game professionally but personally he'd just ended another relationship that had never even got started. Melanie had hit the nail on the head. No heat. No passion. He was beginning to come to the conclusion he might not be capable of it anymore. He didn't think this happened to everyone either. His parents still had love shining out of their eyes when they looked at one another even after all these years. He'd always said he wanted a marriage like theirs but it didn't look like it was in the cards.

There might simply be something wrong with him.

Drained, he stopped to catch his breath, leaning down to rest his hands on his knees. The sweat dripped off his forehead and dropped onto the sidewalk and he lifted the hem of his shirt to wipe his damp face. This run was a good idea. He'd needed a physical challenge, having been stuck to his desk far too often in the last week. Straightening, his gaze fell on the mailbox of the home he was standing in front of. He hadn't realized he'd run so far.

It was Dizzy's house.

He'd run over six miles and he still had to get back home.

Both Dizzy and Leann's cars were in the driveway since the garage was used as an art studio. She'd planted flowers in the window boxes and along the pathway to the front door. A small band of miniature statuettes played in the flower bed near the front door – a puppy whimsically reading a book, a rabbit and her babies pretending to nibble at the leaves, and a pig that simply sat there and smiled. Not a large home, but it looked warm and inviting. It looked like Dizzy. There was a light in the front window and he imagined they were watching a movie or maybe playing a board game. They were both incredibly competitive with one another despite being such close friends.

I've really lost it to end up here.

His gaze turned from Dizzy's house to Trip Stanford's. Easton didn't get the same warm vibe, although there was a light in the window as well. Trip's truck wasn't out front but it might be pulled into the garage. There were no flowers on the walkway, and certainly no garden gnomes on the front lawn. The yard was clipped and maintained but it was more utilitarian in style.

Which didn't make Trip Stanford a killer. It only meant he didn't have a green thumb.

What did you see that night, Dizzy? I know you saw something. What was it?

Chapter Eight

THE MINUTE DIZZY walked into the Anderson house Easton was standing in front of her asking if they could speak. For a moment she thought about making an excuse, telling him she needed to help with dinner in the kitchen, but his expression was so intense that it was clear she wasn't going to get out of this today. It was now or later but it was definitely going to happen. She might as well get it over with so she could have a nice dinner.

She let him lead her upstairs, not sure where they were going but they ended up in Easton's old bedroom, his trophies and ribbons on the wall. He'd been an accomplished baseball player many years ago and might have had a shot at a career but he'd never seemed interested.

"Why don't you sit down?"

The only place to do that was on Easton's old bed. For some reason that seemed like a strange thing to do, although she was pretty sure it had been quite awhile since he'd slept on that mattress. He probably only did it on Christmas Eve when the whole family was together.

Placing her purse on the bed next to her, Dizzy sat down and tried to appear as composed as possible on the few hours of sleep she'd had in the last two days.

"What did you want to talk about?"

Easton didn't sit down, instead looking over her, his hands shoved in the pockets of his blue jeans and his head down, staring at his brown leather shoes. As usual he looked handsome today, if more casual than she usually saw him. Most of the time he was in impeccably tailored suits but today he was in a sinfully well-fitting pair of old jeans and a white button-down shirt, the sleeves rolled up to the elbows.

Stop noticing him. He might look good but he's kind of a jerk.

And he thought she was strange.

He looked up, his blue eyes dark with some emotion she couldn't recognize. Easton had never been easy to read.

"I want to apologize. I mean, really apologize. I've been acting like a total asshole and I don't blame you for telling me to leave Friday night. I'm truly sorry."

He appeared to be completely sincere but she still waited before she replied, wondering if he was going to ruin the apology by tacking on another statement of how she didn't see what she saw.

"Thank you," she finally said, emotion welling up and making it difficult to talk. Easton Anderson hated to apologize and everyone knew it. She didn't have to guess at that since she'd heard him say it more than a few times, and if he didn't willingly acknowledge it his siblings and cousins all reminded him. So this was a big damn deal.

Easton had said he was sorry and it looked like he meant it.

"Something happened that night," Easton went on. "I know

you saw something."

She began to stiffen at his words. *Here it comes...*

"But clearly something very bad happened Friday night, that much I'm sure of, and it wasn't just that you had a nightmare. You saw something."

That wasn't so bad after all. He seemed almost open to her version of events. He didn't believe she saw a murder but perhaps she'd seen Trip attack someone. It was progress.

"Thank you," she said again, not sure how she was supposed to react. Gratitude at this point wasn't an option. She wasn't going to beg for his support. "I know you don't like to apologize so this means a great deal to me."

Chuckling, a smile spread across Easton's face. "You do know me well and yes, I don't like admitting when I'm wrong. Luckily it doesn't happen all that often. It's rare, actually."

Now she was laughing too. He hadn't been down for long, his cocky attitude back and in full force. "We just let you think that to protect your delicate male ego."

"I appreciate it. Now let's get to what's really important. You."

Easton wasn't one who delved into feelings. He was more of a surface-skimming kind of guy.

"What about me?"

"You saw something traumatic. I would imagine it would have an effect."

Was he just playing with her now?

"Since when do you try and psychoanalyze people? You usually leave that to Leann."

He shrugged, his gaze skittering away and then back. "I'm

trying to turn over a new leaf."

She hadn't expected that. "So you're going to try sensitivity and introspection and see how that works for you?"

"Whoa, let's not go too far here." He held his hand up in front of him defensively. "Let's just say I'm trying not to be as much of an asshole and leave it at that."

This was more the Easton she'd known.

"Fair enough. I appreciate your apology and I can say to you honestly that I've barely slept a wink since it happened, but I'm determined to act as normally as possible. Especially as a portion of the town thinks I'm a little eccentric."

But she'd also had many messages of support as well. Thankfully most of Tremont didn't have an opinion one way or the other. They were ignoring the entire situation.

"You don't care what people think."

"I don't," Dizzy agreed without hesitation. "Tami made sure to drill it into my head that I had to be happy with me first and not worry about others. I don't care that some people – like you – think I'm weird. I care that they think I'm lying. That's a whole different thing."

"I never thought you were lying."

Dizzy snorted delicately and then stood, hitching her purse over her shoulder. "No, you just thought I'd imagined it all. As I told you that night, I know you can't help it. It's just the way you are. I shouldn't have told you to leave but I wasn't at my best at that moment. I'm sorry too."

His expression softened. "You don't owe me any apologies. This is all on me."

"What witchcraft is this, Easton? You're being so unusually

humble. It's kind of freaking me out."

"As I said, I'm trying not to be as much of a jerk."

Somehow they'd ended up standing close to one another, just inches between their bodies. The temperature of the room had soared to an almost unbearable level and to make it even worse she could feel the heat coming off of his body. His unmistakably male scent, a combination of citrus and soap, teased her nostrils and her first instinct was to step back, put space between them. Her legs didn't obey.

Instead she found herself staring up into his eyes that didn't look like they normally did. They were bluer, softer, and…something else she couldn't put a name to. Whether it was pity, scorn, or friendship she had no idea. The one thing she knew for sure was that it wasn't lust or desire. She and Easton didn't think about each other like that. They never had. Even when she was a budding teenager and he'd been a suave and sexy older man she hadn't had a crush on him. He simply wasn't her type. She'd crushed on Carter plenty of times but Easton left her cold.

Until now, and this had to be a fluke. Maybe she was coming down with the flu or his mother Andrea had accidentally put the heat on. Delirium would also explain what she'd seen Friday night.

"You're not a jerk," she said when she realized he was waiting for some sort of reply from her. His brows were pinched together with concern and she had to close her eyes for a moment to gather her scattered emotions together. Logical Easton was easy to be around, but this more caring man had her not knowing which way was up. "You're a good person."

Because he was. Like all the Anderson men he was honest, hardworking, and charitable to his community. Okay, sexy as hell too. She could admit that. He'd just been lacking a warmer side.

To her dismay, he reached out and placed a hand on her arm, her skin tingling where he touched. "So are you and I'm sorry that I ever implied that you weren't."

"You didn't. I know you want hard proof. I can't give you that."

It was the way he was wired, which wasn't his fault. The same way Noah liked the physical challenges of running the ranch, Shane liked throwing off the shackles of polite society and going wild, and Carter liked to play the field, basking in female attention. Their little personality quirks made them who they were. It hadn't mattered much until the other night.

Her fingers curled tightly around the soft leather of her handbag, her jumbled senses desperate for some space. Physical space between them.

"I should probably go downstairs and help your mom and aunt with dinner."

His hand dropped away and she breathed a silent sigh of relief. "Did you bake one of your famous cakes for dessert?"

Dizzy always baked a few things when she attended an Anderson Sunday dinner.

"Coconut cake," she said, finally managing to take that step back. "And an apple pie."

"My favorite."

She'd forgotten he'd said that yesterday. Hadn't she?

Chapter Nine

"DID YOU APOLOGIZE to Dizzy?" Carter asked Easton as the Anderson men cleared the table and loaded the dishwasher. It was the tradition that if the women cooked, the men always cleaned up afterward.

"I did," Easton replied, rinsing a dirty pan in the sink. "She graciously accepted. I think we're friends again."

"You should be more than friends with a woman like that," Carter declared, slapping down a stack of dirty plates. "Dizzy's the real deal. The kind of woman that will always be interesting and fun. I don't even know how you stay awake on your dates with Melanie. She's attractive and nice but not exactly scintillating in the conversation department."

This was normally where Easton protested that Dizzy was like a little sister but he couldn't do that anymore. Lately he'd been thinking about things that weren't sisterly in the least.

Most recently when they were upstairs in his childhood bedroom. When he was a teenager he would have given his left nut to have a beautiful woman like Dizzy in his room. A real live female that smelled and looked amazing. Now that he was pushing forty-one he shouldn't have the same reaction but damned if he didn't. He'd been aware of everything about her. The slim fit of her jeans, the way her breasts swelled underneath her pink blouse, and especially how soft her skin was when he'd touched her. Something he should never do again unless she was drowning in the lake or was choking on a bite of food.

Right. Just in emergency situations. He couldn't let her die because she didn't chew her steak sufficiently.

"Hey, Melanie is a lovely woman, so don't say anything against her." Easton elbowed his younger brother out of the way so he could wipe his hands on a dishtowel. "We did end things last night."

His older twin by seven minutes, Noah entered the kitchen juggling a stack of bowls and a couple of glasses. "Who did what to whom last night?"

Waggling his brows, Carter snorted. "East didn't do or get a damn thing. He broke up with his latest girlfriend last night. Again."

Easton didn't need this shit from his younger brother. Or anyone else, for that matter. He had his life firmly in control. For the most part. At least more than Carter had. He'd never spent more than a night or two with any female so he had no room to talk.

"She's a lovely woman. It just didn't work out, that's all. Leave it alone."

But Carter was just getting started.

"Leann and I both think that Easton should ask out Dizzy. What do you think?"

"It doesn't matter what Noah thinks," Easton growled impatiently, nudging his twin aside to place the plates in the dishwasher. He was the only one doing anything to clean up while his brothers stood around with their thumbs up their asses. "My romantic life is not a democracy."

Noah placed the dishes he was carrying on the counter next to the sink. While Easton was the intense and analytical twin, his brother was easygoing and charming, relaxed in a way that Easton actually envied at times.

"Dizzy's a nice girl. You could do worse." Noah laughed and grinned, leaning down to load a stack of silverware into the dishwasher. "As a matter of fact, you have done worse. Remember that–"

"We don't need a trip down memory lane," Easton cut in. "Unless you want to go back and review some of your old girlfriends. There were some real winners in that not-so-exclusive group."

"You're right. But Dizzy is the kind of girl you fall in love with and marry. Why are we discussing this anyway? Has she shown interest in you?"

Not in the least. She probably loathed him at the moment.

Carter, however, was all about this matchmaking nonsense. "There's tension. Major tension when they're in a room together."

"That's because I piss her off," Easton replied heavily, closing the dishwasher door. Anything that didn't fit had to be hand washed and right now he was thinking Shane ought to do it because he hadn't helped at all so far. "It's not because she wants to go out with me."

"But you want to go out with her?" Noah asked, his brow furrowed.

"No, I don't–"

"He doesn't know what he wants," interjected Carter. "His taste in women is questionable at best. He needs to find someone that can't be described as *suitable*."

Dizzy certainly would fit in that category. He doubted she'd enjoy one of the dead boring business events he had to attend on occasion.

Easton was going to kick Shane's ass. They'd not seen hide nor hair of him since the pie had been devoured. Now they were going to get stuck elbow-deep in sudsy water.

"So I should date a witch?"

Noah laughed heartily as he filled the sink. "She's not a witch. She simply has some New Age ideas about the spirit and the body. Remember when I busted my arm last year? She brought over some of those healing crystals and what she called a *candle of intent*. I was supposed to light it every day for a few minutes and picture my arm healed. I figured it couldn't hurt so I did it in the morning when I brushed my teeth and the doctor said I healed faster than anyone he'd ever seen. Said it was, and I quote, miraculous. So who are we to question it? Could be real or it might not but she's not hurting anyone."

"What if she'd told you that you didn't need a cast or pain killers?" Easton challenged.

"I'm open-minded, not crazy," Noah laughed. "Jesus, will you just relax? You're wound tighter than an eight-day clock, as Mom always says. This is why you can't keep a girlfriend. Your taste in women isn't the problem, it's you. You're so much damn work it's exhausting."

Easton wanted to protest, but if there was one person in the world that knew him better than himself it was Noah. They'd grown up together and spent almost every minute of their childhood together. His twin wouldn't lie to him.

"I'm not that bad," Easton muttered, abandoning the dishes and sliding the condiments back into the refrigerator. He was definitely going to kick Shane's ass.

"Dizzy would be a good match for you." Noah began dunking the remaining dishes into the sink to soak. "You're uptight and she's relaxed and peaceful. She could teach you to meditate or some shit like that. And Mom and Dad would be thrilled. They love her like a daughter already."

Carter nodded as he wiped down the counters. "She'd deal with all the Anderson family bullshit well too. She already does so much for the community. She's always volunteering her time for one thing or another and she's deeply involved in the politics of Tremont, understanding the issues. She's passionate about this town as well. After all, she could have stayed in New York City after she graduated from art school but she came home. Add in that she's smart, talented, funny, and beautiful and she's a winner. Hell, if you don't ask her out, I will."

"The hell you will." The words came out before Easton could censure them. "Dizzy is too nice a girl for a playboy like you. Leave her be."

Grinning cockily, Carter just laughed. "I can't imagine how you would have reacted if you were actually attracted to her. Thank goodness she's just a little sister to you."

It was then that Shane decided to join them, the kitchen door swinging open and almost smacking Carter in the face.

"Sorry, I'm late. I got to talking with Mom. What have I

missed?"

Easton picked up a dishtowel and tossed it at his younger brother. "Nothing. Now get to work. We saved the hand washing for you."

Eyes widening, Shane easily caught the rectangle of cloth. "Okay, what's eating you?"

"He broke up with Melanie last night," Carter piped up. "We think he should ask Dizzy out but now I'm thinking I will instead."

"I guess I missed quite a bit," Shane said slowly, his gaze darting between brothers. "And I think I'll keep it that way. Unless East wanted my opinion."

"I don't," Easton said curtly. "And don't call me that."

Easton's mother and West's mother had thought it would be hilarious to have sons named Easton and Westin, born only months apart. It wasn't funny at all.

"Whatever," Shane laughed. "You know you're the only one that is bothered by that name. Everyone else couldn't give a shit. Now Carter, where are you going to take Dizzy?"

"Nowhere. He's taking her nowhere."

Shane's brows flew up and Carter and Noah snickered, not bothering to hide their amusement.

"I think I hit a sore spot. I'll just stay quiet and scrub this pot."

Easton had had it with his siblings. Only Shane was married and the others didn't know anything more about women than Easton did. Hell, probably a lot less.

"I've done my share. Last one out of the kitchen turns on the dishwasher."

Easton turned and exited the kitchen, striding out of the back door and outside to get a lungful of fresh air. He'd apologized, eaten dinner, cleaned up, and now it might be time to go home. Everywhere he turned he couldn't get away from well-meaning family. He knew that Carter wasn't going to ask Dizzy out but he'd taken the bait. He also knew that his brothers and Leann were just wanting to see him happy. They cared about him and it wasn't done to make him crazy, even if that was the actual result. But it also meant that a few awkward conversations were to be had. That's when a terrible thought occurred to him.

If they'd been bugging Easton about Dizzy, had they been talking to her about him? Did she think that he liked her and wanted to ask her out? How did she feel about him and that prospect?

This was worse than fifth grade. Leann might as well pass Dizzy a note asking if she liked Easton. *Check yes or no.* This was why he was a workaholic. He simply didn't get all of this romance stuff. Numbers were safe and predictable. Emotions? They were much more dangerous.

Chapter Ten

TRULY HOT DAYS in Tremont were a rarity. As in hot enough that Dizzy could slip on her bikini and head down to the lake for a cool swim. The weatherman was already saying that a cold front was coming in tonight and the temperature was going to dip again, probably for good. Since she'd had no art classes to teach today she'd decided to take advantage of the sunshine. She'd spent a few hours outside, had a picnic lunch, and now home to take a nap.

She hadn't been sleeping all that well lately despite Leann staying with her.

As she'd loaded up her little economy car before leaving she couldn't help but sneak a glance over at Trip's place. He hadn't been outside much the last few days, only getting in and out of his truck when he left the property. Normally he sat outside on his back patio and read but he hadn't done that either. It looked like he was going to keep to himself, which was fine with her. She'd seen him be cornered by Angela Kincaid just a few houses down yesterday morning when Dizzy was headed to the grocery store. She didn't know what Angela had talked to him about but it probably wasn't the weather or the price of gas because he hadn't looked happy. At least she didn't think he did, but then she'd only caught a glance as she was driving away.

Tired and hot, Dizzy pulled her car into her driveway and cut the engine, retrieving her wet beach towel and picnic basket from the back seat. She was juggling her keys, a half-empty bottle of water, and an overflowing bag when an SUV parked right behind her. She'd managed to lock the car when Easton stepped out of the driver side of the vehicle, looking far too dressed up for such a warm day. His suit was well cut but he had to be roasting in the jacket and tie.

"Did I catch you as you're leaving?"

"No, I just got back from the lake. I had a swim and a little picnic. What brings you by on a Wednesday afternoon? Did you quit your job?"

Normally Easton would be holed up in his climate controlled office buying and selling…well…she really didn't know. She only knew he was really good at it. She'd heard Shane describe Easton as a financial genius.

"I'm still gainfully employed, thank you. Didn't you call my assistant and tell her that you needed me to sign all the participation certificates for the art show? I had a business lunch so I stopped by on my way back to the office."

Dizzy unlocked her front door and motioned Easton to follow her in. With a sigh of relief, she dumped her bag near the door and headed straight for the kitchen.

"I did but I didn't expect you to come to me. I would have brought them to your office." She pulled out a fresh bottle of water. "Want one? It's unusually hot today."

Easton accepted it gratefully. "It sure is. I think it was already snowing last year at this time. Doesn't school start in a few weeks?"

She waved them toward the comfortable sofa and chairs in the living room. "It does but I don't have too much to do to get ready. I just need to set up my student files and organize the new art supplies. Thank you for that, by the way. I'm told that Anderson Industries is the official sponsor of art and music classes in the Tremont school system. How did that happen?"

Drinking down half of the bottle in one go, Easton looked much cooler than he had a few minutes ago. "West is how it happened. You know how the school budgets are tight every year. He came to me and Shane with the idea and we couldn't say no. We know how important art and music are to the curriculum and it's good to give back to the community."

"It is, but…"

She probably shouldn't say what was on her mind.

"But?" he prompted, looking surprised. "You don't think we should have?"

Sighing, Dizzy set her bottle on the coffee table. "You made it too easy for the town council and the school board. They know they can always run to your family to bail them out of whatever stupid thing they did. If art and music are important than the town needs to figure out how they are going to fund those activities. Funny thing, they never seem to have an issue funding sports."

He finished his water and screwed the cap back on. "You know that if we hadn't intervened some teachers might have lost their jobs? One of them could have been you, Dizzy."

"I'm well aware but it still isn't right. The Andersons are always coming to the rescue and you have to be getting tired of it."

Easton shook his head. "It's a privilege to have what we have and this town has been very good to our family. I know everyone thinks that I have a cash register for a heart but I do care about Tremont." He leaned forward so they were eye to eye. "And there was no way I was going to let you get laid off because of budget cuts."

He was close enough that she could feel his warm breath on her cheek. Too close for comfort. The thoughts she'd been having about Easton since dinner on Sunday were disturbing. She'd never thought of him…that way, and in one fell swoop she now couldn't think about anyone else.

"Thank you," she said, an awkward tension in the air that hadn't been there a week ago. "But I know that I'm just a cog in the machine and easily replaceable. It's never a good idea to start thinking that you're irreplaceable."

Easton chuckled, the sound coming from deep in his chest. Had he always laughed this way? "Is that comment directed at me, by any chance? Am I getting a little too big for my britches?"

Dammit, now her attention was pulled to the way the expensive fabric of his pants strained over his powerful thighs and across…

Dear Lord, it is hot in here.

Dizzy took another gulp of her water and then placed the cool bottle on her forehead. She was beginning to feel faint.

Great, now I'm some Victorian virgin with a case of the vapors.

"I'm sure your mother would never allow that," Dizzy replied, her voice coming out shockingly normal despite the turmoil in her belly. "No, it was directed to the universe in general and myself in particular. I just want you to know that I don't expect the Anderson family to rush in and save my job just because Leann and I are friends."

"How about we save it because what you do is important?"

This conversation was going places she hadn't expected.

"Where is Easton Andrew Anderson and what have you done with him?" she demanded in a haughty tone. "You might look like him but you don't act like him."

He finished off the last of his water and laughed. "I'm trying something new."

Don't ask. Don't ask. Don't ask. Have him sign the certificates and leave. Don't flirt.

"Such as?"

I am truly an idiot.

"It has been brought to my attention that I need to be more human, more open, if I don't want to end up alone and bitter telling kids to get off my lawn. My own twin told me I was too much work to be around."

Dizzy's mouth fell open. "Noah said that? Really?"

"Really," Easton confirmed. "So I'm thinking that maybe I need to try and be more like him. More...easygoing and less...what was the word he used? Uptight. I might as well. I was already trying to be less of an asshole."

An image of Easton dressed casually, cutting loose in some local honkytonk with one of Carter's floozies came unbidden into Dizzy's brain and she couldn't get rid of it fast enough. That was the last thing he needed to do.

"I don't think you're uptight."

Chapter Eleven

DIZZY WAS SIMPLY being kind. Easton was well aware that he was uptight, especially compared to his free and easy older twin. Despite running a ranch the size of a small country Noah rarely showed any stress whatsoever, making everything he did look easy.

"You don't have to say that."

Frowning, she slapped her water bottle onto the end table. "I'm not just saying it. You're fine the way you are. Don't let your brothers and cousins make you think that you have to change. Anyone that truly cares for you will accept you as you are."

"Warts and all," Easton added with a grin. "You forgot that part."

"Since when do you have an ego problem? Normally you're cock of the walk, sure of yourself. Even when you should question your judgment, you usually don't."

"Shit, that kind of hurts. Even when I should question myself? I hope that doesn't happen often." From the expression on her face he could tell she was thinking about Friday night. He could have handled the entire situation a hell of a lot better. "I apologized for that."

"You did and I didn't say a word."

"You didn't have to. You're like my mom—every thought she has is right out there for everyone to see. Don't take up poker for a living, sweetheart."

The endearment had slipped out before he could help it but then he remembered calling her something like that when she'd been younger.

"Your mother is a wise and wonderful woman."

Easton would never disagree but he found he liked jousting with Dizzy. She was fun and he'd had little of that lately. Plus, he hoped that perhaps he was getting her mind off of her own issues and problems.

"That wise woman named me Easton at the same time her sister-in-law was naming her son Westin. They thought it was cute. Even your parents wouldn't have done something like that."

Dizzy was openly laughing at him now. "Wow, *even my parents*? That's a hell of a thing to say. I guess Tami and Louis do march to their own drummer, so to speak. But let's remember that my name is Desiree Anastasia. I'm not quite ready to forgive them for that either, so I feel your pain."

He couldn't ever remember anyone calling Dizzy by her real name but he had to admit that she would understand his predicament.

"It's a pretty name," he said. "It…suits you."

A flush crawled up her cheeks making her look even more fetching than she already did in her cutoff jean shorts and plain white blouse. The shorts showed off shapely tan legs and the blouse was unbuttoned just far enough that he could catch a glimpse of her bathing suit top and the curve of a breast, full and ripe. They'd just fit his hands…

Stop. Just stop. This is Dizzy.

"It's a ridiculous name but I guess Dizzy is as well. I bet you think that suits me even better."

It was Easton's turn to be embarrassed. "I don't think that at all."

"I know what everyone thinks about me, so please don't pretend."

It didn't appear to bother her though, and for that he admired her. Dizzy had always lived her life to please herself and no one else. Maybe that was what he should work on instead of trying to be a little more relaxed. Not that either of them came naturally.

He wanted to say this delicately and find the exact right words. "I think it's great that you don't put too much stock in what other people think about you. You do whatever you want to do."

Giggling, Dizzy slapped a hand over her mouth. "Even if what I want to do is strange or weird?"

"Even then."

She tilted her head and studied him for a moment. "And just what do they say about me behind my back? That I howl at the full moon? That I cast spells over the neighbors? Wait…how about that I can read people's minds? I wish I could do that."

"No, you don't," Easton replied immediately. "Didn't you ever see that movie? You definitely don't want to know what others are thinking. I sure as hell wouldn't, especially as most everyone thinks I'm a pain in the ass. And no one thinks you howl at the moon. They might think that you hold séances and talk to the dead, though."

Dizzy's brows pinched together. "Séances? Why would they think that?"

A grin spread across Easton's face. "Because I told them?"

She slapped his arm, her eyes wide with surprise. "Easton Anderson, you did not."

"I didn't." He shrugged but still enjoyed her look of outrage. "I think people just say that you like all the New Age-y stuff like crystals, meditation, yoga."

"Yoga is not new," Dizzy protested. "It's thousands of years old. So is meditation and Eastern medicine. Yoga would help solve that kink in your back. You should try it."

His hand automatically went to his lower back right above the left hip. "How did you know? Did Leann mention it?"

"I could tell by the way you favor it when you sit down and stand up. Yoga would make you feel better. Sitting all day long is slowly killing you."

"That's a cheery thought."

Standing, she took their water bottles into the kitchen and tossed them into the trash. His gaze followed her graceful movements and then lingered on her breasts, pressing against the worn cotton fabric of her blouse. Easton was definitely a boob-man and he'd never noticed Dizzy's before, but now he had to wipe his chin from drooling. He had to concentrate to follow what she was saying when all he wanted to do was explore her bared body.

Focus, man. You're losing it.

"I could show you a few yoga poses that aren't too difficult. You could do them in the privacy of your own home. No one would ever know," she teased, casually leaning a hip against the countertop that separated the two rooms. "Your secret is safe with me. And after all, you're supposed to be trying to loosen up, right? What better way to shut up your brothers than to tell them you've taken up yoga?"

She had a point, although knowing his brothers they'd just give him shit about doing yoga instead. But it was out of his comfort zone...

And damn, he could still hear Carter's voice in his ear declaring that if Easton didn't ask Dizzy out he was going to.

Fuck that.

And Easton kind of wanted another reason to see Dizzy, although he was having a hard time admitting that to himself. This attraction was becoming a nuisance but asking her out might just be the answer. He hadn't met too many women that he liked *more* after spending time with them.

Taking a deep breath, he plunged in to the treacherous waters. This was a terrible idea.

"I'd like that but I do need to get back to the office now. How about I pick you up for dinner later and then you can show me afterward?"

There. He'd done it. He'd asked her out. A pool of sweat had formed on the back of his neck as he waited for her answer. Did she realize what he'd just done? This was a huge shift in their relationship. Seismic. If she said yes, nothing would be the same again.

What the hell have I done?

Stop being so dramatic. When did I become like this?

"We could do that," Dizzy answered slowly, her gaze never leaving his. Her light brown eyes were soft but didn't betray what she might be thinking inside. Maybe she could play poker after all. "What time should I be ready?"

Ready. What a funny word. He'd never be ready to take her on a date but he also couldn't ignore this growing…fascination. Within just a few days she'd turned his world upside down. He was going out on a date with Dizzy Foster and he was going to do yoga. At this point, anything could happen. He might just quit his job, join a motorcycle club, and see the world on the back of a Harley.

That was just as likely as dating Dizzy and yet here he was. Acting completely out of character. This was what happened when he left his office. He was safer at work, safer in an environment he controlled.

Because one thing was for sure…no one could control Dizzy Foster, least of all Easton.

Chapter Twelve

D IZZY DISCARDED ANOTHER wardrobe choice and tossed it on her bed. She hadn't been thinking clearly when she'd accepted Easton's dinner invitation and now she was paying the price. Leann was being no help whatsoever either, simply watching from her perch on the mattress.

"I have nothing to wear," Dizzy wailed to her best friend, pawing through her closet desperately. It was already six-fifteen and she hadn't done her hair or makeup yet either. The most she could say was that she was clean and moisturized after having taken a shower and put on body lotion. "Call your cousin and tell him I came down with appendicitis or maybe the Black Plague. That would keep him away."

Brows raised, Leann briefly checked her phone. She was waiting for Zach to come over and spend the night. "The Black Plague? I didn't realize we had a rat problem in Tremont. Seriously though, Easton is not even going to notice what you're wearing. He's not the type unless you're wrapped up in nothing but a profit and loss statement and high heels. Wear anything you want."

"You're not helping," Dizzy growled, tugging at the neckline of a dark purple dress in the back of her closet. Tami had given it to her one year for her birthday but Dizzy had never worn it. The weather was usually too chilly for a sleeveless dress made of silk but not tonight. "What about this?"

Leann stood and took the hanger from Dizzy, checking out the dress back and front. "This will look amazing on you. How come I've never seen this before? Is it new?"

"Tami gave it to me as one of my birthday presents a few years ago but it's usually not warm enough to wear it, and when it was I didn't have anyplace to go."

"I think you should wear it," Leann pronounced. "I have no idea where he's taking you but you'll wow him for sure. Just…don't have too high of expectations for this evening. I don't want you to be disappointed."

Now the search for suitable undergarments was next. Dizzy pulled out a drawer and began to rifle through stacks of panties and bras. "I don't know what you mean. Why would I be disappointed? I thought you said that you encouraged Easton to ask me out."

That had been shocking news when Dizzy had told Leann she had a date with her cousin tonight. Apparently, a few of the Anderson siblings were pushing this match. That explained why he'd asked in the first place of course. It wasn't because he was awestruck with loving and passionate feelings every time he looked at her or anything. Because of that it was silly to worry and fuss as much as she was about her hair and clothes but it wasn't in her nature to do anything halfway. If she was going on a date – with Easton or any other man – she wanted to look her best and have a lovely time.

But also because she was attracted to Easton. She couldn't pretend that what she'd been feeling the last few times they'd been together didn't exist. Honestly, he was the last person she'd expected to feel this way about but she was also curious to see where it led. It could be great, but honestly it was probably going to be a disaster. They looked at life so differently.

"I did encourage him, as did Carter and Shane. I think you'd be good for Easton and help him loosen up a bit, but you know how he is," Leann replied, settling back on the bed. "He's difficult to be around at the best of times. He'll probably bore the living shit out of you tonight talking about Dow Jones Industrial Averages and Price-Earnings ratios. Just be sure to drink lots of caffeine so you can stay awake."

Dizzy wasn't going to let Leann talk about her cousin that way. Easton was a good man and she'd never been bored.

"Not nice," Dizzy admonished, giving her friend a stern look. "What a way to talk about your own flesh and blood. Easton is a sweet person and never has he tried to talk to me about Bob Jones Industrials or whatever they're called. If anything, we usually talk about his family or my art."

Leann squirmed, her face pink. "Dow Jones, and I'm sorry. You're right but he does do that at work."

"Of course he does." Dizzy held up a pair of silk and lace panties with a matching bra. "He's at work. Eureka! I found them. Now I'm going to get dressed. If Easton comes to the door please let him in. And be nice too."

"I'm his cousin. I'm not supposed to be nice," Leann called after Dizzy who was already in the bathroom. She had about thirty minutes to finish getting ready because knowing Easton as she did, he would be perfectly on time. Not a second late. Time was money and all that.

As unbelievable as it was, Dizzy was going on a date with Easton Anderson. By tomorrow morning, the gossip mill would be buzzing about them whether it be good, bad, or indifferent. Half of the town would have them in a mad, passionate affair and the other half would say that they ended the evening in a huge argument, vowing never to speak to one another again.

Which one was going to be right?

✦　✦　✦

SO FAR, THE date hadn't been a complete disaster. There'd been a tense moment when the waiter had recommended the veal to Dizzy. Holding his breath, Easton had waited for her lecture to the poor guy, but she must have thought better of it in this more upscale establishment because she simply redirected the waiter to another spot on the menu, asking about the gnocchi.

She'd ended up ordering the cheese lasagna while he'd settled on the chicken Milanese.

Easton had ordered a fruity wine to pair with their meal and the waiter, who filled their glasses with a flourish, also dropped off a basket of breads before scurrying back to the kitchen.

Dizzy lifted her glass to her glossy lips and took a sip. Why did he suddenly find her mouth so mesmerizing? "This was a great choice. I love the food here."

It had taken a full hour to decide on this place. His other picks were either too casual or too fussy. He was trying to make this date look effortless on his part but he wasn't sure it was working all that well.

"Thank you."

Jesus, they'd run out of conversation already and the salads hadn't even arrived yet. He was officially sweating through his expensive button-down shirt.

On the other hand, Dizzy looked calm, cool, and collected. And gorgeous too. Dressed in a plum-colored sleeveless dress that lovingly clung to each and every curve as if it had been made just for her, she certainly didn't have him thinking about little sisters. Tonight she'd coiled her long chocolate colored hair up into a knot and it showed off her graceful neck and delicate jawline. When he'd picked her up, he'd almost swallowed his own tongue. She was that sexy.

So now he was nervous as hell, barely knowing what to say or do. Leann had pulled him aside and warned him not to bore Dizzy all night with talk of financial deals. She'd told him that he should ask about his date. But the problem was, he'd known Dizzy for years. Were there things he didn't know? Probably, but how to ask about them? He was used to dates where they didn't get all that personal.

"Thank you for stopping by to sign all of those certificates," Dizzy said. "That was extremely thoughtful of you. Now I can give them out on Friday when I teach classes again."

"It was no trouble," he assured her again, grateful that she'd brought up a topic they both agreed on. "It was actually a nice break in the day. Half the time I don't even stop for lunch."

Smiling, she took another sip of her wine. "The busy executive. You said you were at a business lunch. Anything interesting? Or is it a secret?"

"Is anything a secret in this town?" he laughed. "It's nothing that exciting. A townhome development that we're working on but not here in Tremont. It's in Douglas, about a hundred miles from here."

Once again he held his breath, waiting for her to say something negative. He knew quite well how she felt about cookie cutter housing. That's why she'd bought that house in the cul de sac. She'd said it had *character and history,* which Easton took to mean that it needed thousands of dollars in renovations. He had to admire her, though, because she'd done a great deal of the work herself, only using help for the flooring.

"You're a busy man. Would you be jealous to know that I took a nap this afternoon?"

"Incredibly jealous," he laughed. "I don't remember the last time I took a nap. I might have been in preschool."

She pretended to be shocked, her eyes going wide and her mouth falling open. "Then you need to put that on your bucket list right away. There's nothing like taking a nap to the sound of rain on the roof. It's a must-do."

"Bucket list?" he groaned. "I'm not much older than you are."

Until a few days ago, ten years had felt like a damn long time but it really wasn't all that bad. They weren't kids, after all.

Not that this relationship was going to go anywhere. It was only a date. Just dinner. And maybe yoga later. In fact, there was no relationship at all except that she was a friend of the family. An incredibly sexy friend.

"You don't need to be old to have a bucket list. I have one."

The waiter slid their salads in front of them so Easton had to wait a moment to respond, but he absolutely had to know what was on her list. He'd bet it was a doozy. Carter had been right about one thing – Dizzy was never a bore.

"I must hear what's on this list. What does Desiree Foster want to do before she leaves this earth?"

Rolling her eyes, she dug into the leafy greens on her plate. "I doubt any of it would interest you all that much. You'd probably just laugh."

"I promise I won't laugh."

Placing her fork on the edge of her plate, she gave him an appraising look. Clearly she had her doubts. "I know that you think I'm a little...*squirrelly,* so it might be foolhardy to make that claim without first knowing what's on the list. What if I said I wanted to meet an alien being?"

"Do you?"

He didn't believe in alien encounters but if he did he would want to meet one. He might be able to learn something and he loved learning new things.

She slapped her hand on her forehead. "No, I do not. It was just an example."

"I'm not laughing," he pointed out. "Do you believe in life on other planets?"

Easton couldn't believe how easily they were conversing after getting off to such a slow start but then he shouldn't have been surprised. He and Dizzy had never had a problem talking. Or disagreeing. He'd told himself not to speak about anything controversial so they wouldn't get into a debate but he was beginning to think that there was no way to do that. Digging into Dizzy's brain and seeing how it worked was half the fun of being with her. No one else's mind worked quite the way hers did.

She tapped her chin as she thought about his question. He liked that she was taking it seriously. "I'd like to believe it because that would be fascinating. I haven't really studied up on the subject so I don't know if there's evidence either way. I think that since there is life on this planet there is a decent chance that another planet might have life as well, but who knows how far away they are? I doubt we'll know in my lifetime."

A well-thought out argument.

"I'd like to believe too."

Her brows raised and she smiled. "You would? That's quite an admission, Easton."

"I'm full of surprises."

That had her laughing out loud. "Are you? That's a surprise in and of itself but I look forward to learning about all these hidden facets about you."

"It's going to be a real treat," he teased. "Now seriously, what's on that bucket list?"

This evening was turning out better than he'd ever believed possible.

Chapter Thirteen

DIZZY TOOK ANOTHER bite of the decadent chocolate
mousse and hummed in appreciation. Easton appeared to
be enjoying it as well if the smile on his face was anything to go
by. Thankfully they were sharing or she'd eat it all by herself and
then she'd have to waddle out of the restaurant, satisfied but far
too full and feeling miserable the rest of the evening.

Easton took another spoonful. "It's almost as good as one of
your desserts."

Sputtering, she almost choked with laughter. "Are you kid-
ding? This is fantastic and was probably made by a professional
pastry chef. I'm just a lowly home baker."

"Who makes terrific apple pies. Seriously, I love your cooking."

The date had gone well so far. Why not step out on a limb
and see how he was feeling? It was better to find out now than
later.

"Maybe next time I'll make dinner for us. I know you love a
good pot roast."

She gave a mental sigh of relief at his boyish grin of delight.
Clearly, he liked the idea.

"You'd make me pot roast?"

He was acting like she'd offered him one of her kidneys. It was a piece of meat. She'd throw it in the slow cooker and ignore it for eight hours. No magic involved.

"And potatoes, carrots, and gravy."

"I'm not going to say no to that."

A shadow fell over the table before Dizzy could respond and she looked up to find a smiling and well-dressed couple around Easton's age standing there.

"Easton," the man exclaimed to her date, but his gaze had slid over to her. Looking her up and down, appraising and measuring. Dizzy didn't like it one bit. She had an instinct about people and this one wasn't anyone she would trust as a friend. "So good to see you. How long has it been? Six months at least."

"At least," Easton replied smoothly. "I haven't been playing golf lately. Shoulder injury. Dizzy, let me introduce you to Gary and Alicia Jones. They're members at the club. Gary and Alicia, this is Desiree Foster. She teaches art at the school and also volunteers at the community center."

Gary Jones. She recognized his name from the newspapers. He was some big deal at the bank, which explained how Easton knew him.

He was also slimy, giving her a lecherous look right in front of his wife and so-called friend.

Extending her hand, she steeled herself to be touched by this worm. "It's so nice to meet you."

Gary held her hand a little too long and his wife's fingers were freezing. Jeez, these were what passed for friends in Easton's world? No wonder he stayed in his office and worked. It explained everything.

Alicia's fake smile was chilly also. "Desiree Foster? Aren't you the woman that called in that fake murder to the police last week?"

Well, damn. Dizzy would have thought well-bred rich people wouldn't be rude enough to bring that up but not this couple. The wife looked like she was enjoying the hell out of this. She'd probably dine out on this for weeks because she'd met Dizzy in person.

I can only imagine the crap she'll make up too.

"Dizzy saw something, Alicia. She didn't make it up."

Easton had that tone in his voice that didn't invite arguing.

"I'm sure she did," Alicia replied, her eyes blue chips of ice. She leaned down so that only Easton and Dizzy could hear and the smell of whiskey permeated the air. "The rumor around town is that you had a little too much to drink over a broken love affair. It's alright, dear. We all do it now and then."

That's what was going around town? People really needed to get a hobby.

Easton's eyes narrowed and a muscled ticked in his jaw as he nodded toward the swaying woman. "I think your wife has had a few too many, Gary. You might want to take her home."

Gary must have had a couple of cocktails too because he didn't seem to notice the edge in Easton's tone. "We're just having some fun tonight. It's all between friends."

Except that Dizzy wasn't their friend and she couldn't imagine why Easton was.

"Go home, Gary, and sleep it off."

This time the man seemed to get the message, lurching to

the side of his wife and wrapping an arm around her waist, whether for emotional support or because he was feeling woozy, Dizzy had no idea.

"You've always had a big stick up your ass, Anderson. You're just no fun."

Easton nodded in agreement, his attitude decidedly frosty. "That's true. Have a nice evening. You might want to let the hostess call you a taxi."

The offending couple walked off and the air around Easton and Dizzy immediately felt less tense and a whole lot happier, but there was still tension in the air. Those two weren't exactly spreading sunshine and unicorns.

An awkward silence fell over the table. Dizzy didn't know what she was supposed to say and apparently Easton didn't know either. It went on for a couple of minutes until their excuse for not speaking – the chocolate mousse – was gone. They couldn't continue their evening like this. She pointed at Easton, determined to make light of the situation. "You're a taxi."

His brow wrinkled and he shook his head, clearly confused. "What? I don't understand."

Of course he didn't. He was far too intelligent to get a laugh at a dumb joke.

"It's an old joke," Dizzy explained. "I was trying to break the tension. You told them to have the hostess call them a cab. *You're a cab.* She called them a cab. Get it? It's just a stupid joke."

Now she felt stupid but then Easton smiled. The tension was officially broken. "I've never heard that one before."

Dizzy feigned shock, her hand flying to cover her open

mouth. "How is this possible? That joke is older than our parents and it's not even that funny."

"I don't know, it's kind of cute." His entire demeanor had changed since his friends had left. He'd gone from cold and remote to warm and endearing. "When you tell it, anyway."

A flush of heat suffused her cheeks and she tried to play it off by sipping her water.

"Interesting friends you have. I have a feeling they're going to be talking about me…and you…to everyone in your little social group."

Reaching across the table, he captured her hand, his thumb softly stroking her pulse point. It should have felt strange and disturbing – this was Easton after all – but instead it simply felt right. Like he should have been doing it for years.

"They are definitely not my friends and I don't belong to any social group that includes them. I see them from time to time at parties and at the club. I'm cordial because we do business together but frankly, I find them boring as hell. After tonight, I also find them ill-mannered and cruel. So my next question is…are you okay? Should I have punched Alicia out for what she said?"

The image of Easton defending her honor with a right hook to Alicia's chin made her smile, although she knew it was wrong. Wrong, wrong, wrong. Physical violence was never the answer. But as this was only pretend Dizzy gave herself a break. Just this once.

Although she wouldn't mind if Alicia had a nasty hangover tomorrow.

"That might not be the best idea but I appreciate the sentiment. I'm fine. I don't care about their opinion of me, although I have to admit that it's interesting to hear one of the stories that's going around town. I bet that's one of the tamer ones."

"I'm still sorry they acted that way. I'm mortified by their behavior and why they thought it was okay to do that. They're crass and snooty but they've never been downright rude like that."

"To your social circle," she pointed out. "But I'm just one of the unwashed masses. I bet they're crappy to wait staff too. People like that always are. And that's not your fault, but thank you for the unnecessary apology. None of this was your fault."

Dizzy had always felt that a person could tell quite a bit about someone by how they treated those in food service. Having waited tables in New York on the upper West side while she was in art school, she knew what a thankless job it was. Hard on the back, hard on the feet, and the abuse from nasty customers had almost made her quit several times. Luckily there were many more nice people in the world than mean ones.

"Actually, I think you're right," Easton agreed. "I've seen them both berate a waiter or a parking valet for taking too long."

"I've got a good eye when it comes to people. I follow my intuition and it's rarely wrong. The minute Gary came up to the table and looked at me I knew he wasn't a good person."

"That was quick. You don't think you jump the gun when you do that? Not that you weren't right this time," he added hastily.

She wasn't surprised that Easton wasn't a fan of her methods. "I trust my gut more than a spreadsheet of numbers. Just because something, or someone in this case, looks good on paper doesn't mean that they are. How long did it take you to figure out that Gary and Alicia were kind of terrible people?"

Shifting in his seat, his cheeks turned red. "Not long. He was difficult to work with and I had to ask for certain documents multiple times. As for Alicia, I've seen her at the club and I don't think I've ever seen a genuine smile from her."

"That's sad. You have to wonder if she's a happy person. Life's too short, you know? But it sounds like you and I came to the same conclusion but used slightly different methods. But I bet ultimately you trusted your instincts. They're just not your go-to method."

He hadn't let go of her hand and he took possession of the other one, his large hands enveloping her much smaller ones. There was something about Easton, a way he had that made her feel protected and cared for. Not that she needed him to. She didn't. But it was a nice, comfortable feeling even if she had no business feeling it.

"And what does your intuition tell you about me?" Easton asked, his voice deep and throaty. A bolt of electricity ran up her spine and she had to take a few breaths before she could answer.

"That you're a good man." She giggled at his look of pride. "A frustrating one, too, but a good one."

And that fact was becoming a big problem. She'd never expected to have this good of a time with Easton. But she had and more. He was smart, funny, sexy, and a just a nice man. He was also the cousin of her best friend.

What in the heck was she supposed to do now?

✦　✦　✦

EASTON WAS INSTANTLY on alert when he and Dizzy walked into her house and found Leann pacing back and forth while her boyfriend Zach peered out the kitchen curtains, a frown on his face. Zach was usually pretty laid back and happy, especially in Leann's presence, so his mood didn't bode well.

Leann rushed over to Dizzy and gave her a hug. "I'm so glad you're home. You won't believe what he's doing now."

Everyone needed to get a grip. His cousin was pale and clearly shaken so he turned his attention to Zach, who looked to be the calmer of the two.

"What's going on? What are you watching?"

Turning from the window, Zach rubbed at his temple. "Our good friend Trip Stanford has decided to put in a flowerbed in his back yard. He's been out there for a couple of hours."

Easton wasn't getting what Zach was trying to say but then he was a humble finance guy who didn't deal with murder and mayhem every day.

"Can you translate that for me?"

Leann had slapped down two wine glasses on the kitchen counter and poured them half full. "I can do that. Trip Stanford is putting a flowerbed in his back yard. In Montana at the end of summer. Under the cover of darkness. Do you see where we're going with this now?"

Fuck.

Dizzy reached for one of the glasses and took a gulp. "This is good though, right? I mean, we'll catch him red-handed when he tries to bury the body."

We? Easton didn't like the sound of that. If a killer was burying a body, his pretty female neighbor probably shouldn't be hanging around watching.

"You're not going anywhere near Trip Stanford."

He hadn't meant for the words to come out so bossy but if it kept her inside the house he didn't care.

Her brows shot up to her hairline. "Are you giving me an order? Because let me tell you what you can do with—"

"Can I get some quiet here?" Zach interrupted loudly. "Let's not tip him off that we're watching him. I think he saw you leave for the evening with Easton so he thinks that you're not at home, Dizzy. Plus, Leann and I just got here about half an hour ago. That's why he's chosen tonight."

"That and the smell," Leann muttered under her breath. "Unless he had her in a freezer it had to be getting bad."

They'd all watched too many horror movies. But this was high on the creep factor if Stanford was truly out there burying a dead body.

"Morbid much?" Easton asked as his cousin. "Dizzy just ate dinner. Have some sensitivity."

Dizzy, however, waved away his concern. "My stomach is fine but my heart is racing a mile a minute. Should we call the cops?"

Zach shook his head, his lips a grim line. "Gardening it not against the law and considering that they don't believe you right now, I think it might be the worst thing we could do. Currently your friendly neighborhood murderer thinks he's gotten away with it. We need to let him continue to think that. Otherwise he might turn his attention to you...and Leann by extension."

Easton had placed a reassuring hand on Dizzy's back and he could feel the shudder that ran through her body at Zach's statement. She was frightened but he wasn't going to allow anyone or anything to hurt her. Trip wouldn't get within fifty feet of Dizzy and Easton would make sure of it.

Lifting the curtain slightly, Easton peeked out of the window and across to Stanford's back yard. Just as Zach and Leann had said, a single light shown on the deck. Perhaps it was a lantern or a bright flashlight, but it cast a beam of light down the steps and into the yard where a lone dark figure was hunched over with a shovel planting flats of flowers into the ground.

"What did you see? Did you see him bury the body?"

Easton felt a hand on his arm and turned to see Dizzy looking up at him, her eyes wide with surprise. "Then you believe me?"

The choice was clear in front of him. Two roads. But his path was easy to see.

"I do," he said firmly. "Now we have to figure out what to do about it."

Because he wouldn't let her become victim number two.

Chapter Fourteen

D IZZY'S HAND VISIBLY shook as she set the wine glass down
on the table. She'd had a few sips but it was better to keep
a clear head. The time for getting tipsy clearly wasn't now. Her
neighbor had just buried a dead body in his backyard. They just
hadn't caught him in the act. By the time Leann and Zach had
shown up, Trip had been planting flowers on top.

And Easton believed her that it had happened.

Sure, the fact that Zach and Leann weren't questioning her
sanity might have had something to do with it. Or the fact that
Trip Stanford was currently knee deep in dirt in the dark. That
was suspicious all on its own. Still, Easton believed that she'd
witnessed a murder. This was real growth for him. He hadn't
seen it with his own eyes and it was something hard to believe in
the first place. There was no evidence to point to, no other
witnesses. Somehow though he'd mustered the courage to go
beyond his five senses and that was big. If she hadn't heard it
from his own mouth she wouldn't have believed it.

Easton and Zach were looking out of her kitchen windows
while she and Leann sat at the table. Dizzy's legs had felt decidedly like jelly but she was beginning to recover from the shock of

the news. Just what was Trip thinking?

He's thinking that no one believes you.

"So walk me through what you saw when you got here," Easton said, his gaze still zeroed in on the single spotlight in Trip's backyard. "Was he digging the hole?"

"He'd already dug the hole and was planting the flowers," Zach replied. "But it was pitch dark outside and had been for some time. No way he started when it was light out. Plus, there's no moon tonight which I'm sure helps him."

Gray clouds had filled the sky since late afternoon but tomorrow was supposed to dawn clear. And cold. The weatherman had said that the warm temperatures were behind them and the chilly air of fall was back for good.

"It makes no sense to plant flowers the last night of summer, right?" Dizzy asked, amazed that the entire town didn't see what she did. "I mean…there's no logic there. They're going to freeze and die."

"I've seen it snow in July," Leann declared. "So yes, they're going to die eventually. But even if it was June it doesn't make a lick of sense to plant them in the dark."

"Unless you're trying to hide something. Then it's perfectly logical." Easton dropped the curtain. "He's going back inside so I guess he's done. Now what do we do?"

"We can't call the police," Leann sighed. "They don't believe that anything happened."

Zach turned from the window and went to stand behind Leann, massaging her shoulders.

"And they can't dig up his yard without a warrant anyway. We didn't actually see him bury anything. He'd just say that it's no crime to plant pretty flowers."

Dizzy was still having a hard time comprehending what had gone on here tonight.

"It's so brazen. It's like he's taunting me. He knows I know and he knows that no one thinks I'm telling the truth."

"That's not true," Leann protested. "We believe you, and it's only a matter of time before everyone does."

Easton hadn't said much tonight, his expression thoughtful and angry at the same time.

"Do you think people will eventually believe me?" Dizzy asked him. "If nothing changes and we don't have any proof?"

"We have to get proof," he said after a quiet pause. "But that's not exactly my department. I think we need to keep a close eye on him, though. He might eventually slip up and show his cards."

They might be waiting forever for that.

"And in the meantime?" Dizzy questioned. "Is he going to keep messing with me?"

Zach shook his head. "First off, I don't think he meant for you to see that tonight. My theory is he saw you leave with Easton and took the opportunity. It was his bad luck that you didn't go anywhere after dinner and came straight home. I think he was counting on you seeing a movie too."

Leann's brows pulled down. "So you don't think he's taunting her?"

"I don't but I could be wrong. This whole situation doesn't feel like he's an experienced killer. He did it in his own home, first off. That's a big no-no."

"Gacy and Dahmer did it in their own homes," Easton

pointed out, leaning a hip against the counter. "It's not unheard of."

"That's true," Zach conceded. "But this one doesn't feel planned. He got the female here. We know that."

"And she didn't drive her own vehicle," Easton added. "Maybe they were on a date?"

"That's a good guess," Zach agreed. "They were on a date and things went well enough that she said yes to coming to his place. That's a lot of trust for a woman to put in a man. My guess would be that it wasn't their first date."

"They could have met online," Dizzy said. "One of the teachers at school does a lot of online dating and she talks to them for weeks or even months before she meets them. She always says she feels like she knows them really well."

"Then she'd trust them," Leann nodded. "Enough to maybe even go home with them. So you don't think he planned it?"

"If he did, he's lousy at it," Zach snorted. "He didn't think about the neighbors or making noise or being seen. He had no method of disposing the body and no alibi other than he was home all alone and asleep."

That was pretty lame. If Dizzy was planning to murder someone she'd make sure that she had a dozen people as her alibi.

"So the good news is that I don't probably have a serial killer as a neighbor," Dizzy said. "The bad news is that he might have anger issues and poor impulse control, plus a healthy disrespect for the female gender."

Zach placed a kiss on Leann's cheek. "Jared's working on the background check for Trip Stanford. Once we have that we can see if there are any skeletons in his closet. It will also give me something more to go on to build a profile. Other than that, we need to keep an eye on him and keep you safe." He gave Dizzy a smile. "Both of you."

Should she be worried about her safety? Would he come after her at some point?

"Seriously, would he try anything? If he did the cops would look at him first."

Zach nodded in agreement. "That's true but eventually all the gossip will die down and he'll start to feel comfortable. Except for one outstanding thing. You. He may decide that he can get away with getting rid of you. He's already killed once and right now is getting away with it. That's going to breed confidence inside of him."

Easton crossed his arms over his chest, a determined glint in his blue eyes. "Then we need to make sure to shake that confidence. Make sure he knows we're still watching and talking about it. Keep up the pressure."

"I agree up to a point." Zach pointed to Easton and them himself. "You and I need to keep up the pressure. These ladies? They need to fade into the background."

Dizzy wasn't a happy camper when people were talking about her like she wasn't sitting right there.

"Um…you know we're in the same room, right?" She held up her hand like she was in a classroom waiting to be called on by the teacher. "It is my life. I get a say in this."

Easton opened his mouth but she shut him down immediately before he could get started, poking her finger into his chest.

"You know I'm right and that you'd do the same, so don't

even go there."

Sighing, he nodded. "Fine. You get to decide. Do you want to live or die? It's your choice."

She turned to Leann, who was watching with great interest. "He's a charmer, isn't he? And they say he has no people skills."

"I have people skills. Shit. They don't say that. They say I'm cold and heartless. Two totally different things."

His indignant tone almost had her laughing but the situation didn't exactly lend itself to levity.

"I'm sure you do," she said in her most soothing tone. "And you're not cold and heartless either."

If she'd ever thought he was – and she had to admit that there were times when she did – she certainly couldn't say that now. He'd shown a far different side of himself these last few days. A side she was becoming quite enamored of.

"I'm going to stay here tonight again," Zach pronounced. "But I'm going to need to leave for an out of town assignment tomorrow. Do you think you could stay here while I'm gone?"

Easton nodded as if it was a foregone conclusion, but to Dizzy it wasn't by a longshot. This wasn't technically his battle. He'd only been dragged into it because he'd driven Leann here Friday night.

The men quietly talked, making plans or whatever it was that men did, while Leann and Dizzy looked out the kitchen window to Trip's yard. They couldn't help themselves. There wasn't much to see but the whole situation was grotesque and she felt nauseous simply thinking about it.

"Dizzy, can you walk me to my car?"

Following Easton outside, she wanted to say something to

him but she wasn't sure how to word it. She didn't want to come off as ungrateful but she also didn't want him to feel like he had to protect her when it wasn't his responsibility.

"Thank you for dinner," she said, standing next to the driver's side door. The air had turned cool and goosebumps covered her arms while a tension had taken up residence between them. It wasn't awkward or unwelcome but it was definitely *there,* almost a living, breathing entity that stood between them. But if she reached out to touch it she would only find her hand on his chest.

Would that be so bad?

"You're welcome. How about we spend the day together tomorrow? Maybe go for a ride on the ranch?"

Dizzy wanted to spend more time with him and he seemed to feel the same. But first they needed to get something straight.

"That sounds like fun but…"

"But?" he prompted. "You don't sound too sure."

Taking a deep breath, she plunged in. "This isn't your fight, Easton. I know how the Anderson men are. I've spent most of my life with you all. But protecting me isn't your job. Until about twenty-four hours ago you didn't even think there was anything to protect me from."

"I do now."

His expression gave nothing away and she was damn good at reading people. *He* could probably take up poker for a living.

"Yes, but it's still not your responsibility. Zach is protecting Leann because they have a relationship."

That tension had built to the point she could barely breathe in oxygen and she was beginning to get lightheaded. Easton, on the other hand, didn't look perturbed in the least, simply smiling widely before sliding his arms around her waist and pulling her close to his warm body. If she'd been cold a second ago, now she was burning up.

"A man protects the woman in his life." Easton bent his head, his lips hovering just over hers. She couldn't see his eyes well in this light, but she had a feeling they were that soft dark blue instead of like ice earlier when they'd met his sort of friends. His hands had splayed out on her lower back and he was urging her even closer until her breasts were pressed tightly between them. "I like you, Dizzy."

If she hadn't known Easton Anderson her whole life she would have thought his revelation no big deal. Nothing to see here, folks. But she of all people knew that he'd just revealed a bombshell.

He liked her. And that wasn't something he went around saying to every girl.

She had to swallow hard to be able to speak through the lump that had taken up residence in her throat. "I like you too."

His lips on hers was his reply. He was tender but in control, his mouth questioning, seeking, but not tentative either. And damn, did he know how to kiss. She'd heard rumors, of course, about all the Anderson boys but somehow she hadn't thought of Easton that way. Maybe it was something in their genes. A giggle rose up in her throat at her wayward thoughts.

Lifting his head, Easton smiled indulgently. "What's so funny? Do I kiss wrong?"

Shaking her head, she had to cling to his shoulders to stay upright. He'd kissed her until her knees had given out. "Not in the least. It's just…I'm happy."

His fingers brushed her cheek. "I'm happy too. Now about tomorrow?"

"What about work?" she asked as he trailed his lips across her jaw. She had to stifle the groan but she couldn't do a thing about the bar of arousal that was building in her abdomen. All from a few kisses. Clearly, she'd been too long between dates.

"I have exactly one hundred and sixty vacation days that I have not taken and HR – that's Leann – is always bugging me to take them but I never had a good reason. I do now."

Heat swept through her cheeks at his intimation. She was that good reason. It felt nice to be wanted. Tami might lecture her about getting involved with such a strong-minded male but Dizzy liked that Easton didn't roll over and play dead. He had thoughts and opinions of his own. They could debate and discuss, then still be friends.

Or lovers.

That too. Maybe.

And then he was kissing her again and all logical thought fled her brain and she was operating on emotion only. Never had she been so swept away by the meeting of mouth on mouth but one touch from this man and she became a blithering idiot.

"I have to go. I'll call you in the morning. Let me know if anything else happens tonight."

He stepped back and she immediately felt the loss of his body heat. His fingers trapped a strand of her hair and he tucked it behind her ear, stroking her jaw as he did so. With a shaky breath, she bid him goodbye and a safe trip home. Watching his taillights disappear into the night, she tried unsuccessfully to get her racing heart under control.

Easton.

He was the last person she would ever have imagined would make her feel this way. But now that she did? She didn't want it to end.

Chapter Fifteen

IT MIGHT HAVE been more romantic to horseback ride around the Anderson ranch but Dizzy seemed to be enjoying the ATV Easton had pulled out of the barn. Her arms were wrapped tightly around his waist and her laughter was like music to his ears with every hill and dip. Her perfect breasts were pressed against his back, inspiring more than a few naughty fantasies that he shouldn't be having about his cousin's best friend.

Oh well. I'm going to enjoy them.

He couldn't remember the last time he'd taken the day off of work and just had fun. Usually he dragged his laptop and cell phone with him like a life preserver as if Anderson Industries would implode if he stopped watching. This the most liberated he'd felt in ages and it was all because of Dizzy. There was something about her that encouraged him to leave his comfort zone behind and stake out new territory. With her, the status quo simply wasn't good enough. He wanted to take it to the next level no matter what they were doing.

Which made it all the more ironic that he felt so comfortable in her presence. Kissing her had certainly not felt strange in the least. It had felt…right. But within that comfort was excitement and passion as well. So strange that the two could live so easily together. Life didn't have to be boring but it didn't have to be a roller coaster every single minute either.

Pulling up to the stream at the back of the property, he parked the ATV under a large shade tree and swung his leg over before tugging off his helmet. Dizzy's came next, her long hair spilling out of her ponytail and over her shoulders and back. Like a punch in his gut, he couldn't stop from staring at the beautiful picture she made. Her cheeks were pink with excitement and her light brown eyes sparkled with delight. He didn't even have a chance to stow their helmets before she threw her arms around him, placing a kiss next to his mouth. His skin tingled where she'd pressed her lips. Jesus, he was like a teenager out with the prom queen.

"That was fantastic," Dizzy crowed, her voice a little dry from the wind. "This was a much better idea than horses. I want to do that every day of my life."

"Easy, honey," Easton chuckled. "That might be overkill, but we can definitely do this often if you want to."

He sent that idea up like a trial balloon, hoping she didn't see it for what it was – the hopeful suggestion that this relationship could be a thing. An ongoing one. Not just a few dates and then they'd drift apart. He wanted to see where this might go.

Was that completely insane? A week ago he thought Dizzy was – at the very least – eccentric. Now he was seeing her in a whole new light. She was creative and beautiful and kind. People and animals adored her. So what if she walked in the rain to cleanse her soul? It was only water. His soul could probably use a good scrub.

"I'm going to hold you to that, Easton Anderson." She scrambled away from the ATV and stood at the banks of the stream. Bending down, she stuck her fingers into the water before gasping and jerking them back as if she'd touched a hot stove. But he knew from experience that water was anything but warm. "Holy Mother Nature, that water is freezing. It's not fit for humans."

And yet all the Anderson siblings and cousins had jumped in to cool off after working long, hot days on the ranch. Not that they'd stayed in long. They would have turned blue.

"How have you known our family all these years and never gone for a swim? How is that even possible?"

Wiping the water on her soft and worn blue jeans, she climbed up onto a rock to stare down into the crystal clear water. From there she should be able to see all the way to the bottom.

"Because every summer Tami and Louis dragged me on whatever trip they had planned," she reminded him. "They said they wanted to expand my mind and be aware of the world outside of Tremont."

He stood behind her and placed his hands on her hips to hold her steady. He'd seen a few people slide right off that rock and into the cold water. "Did it work?"

Glancing over her shoulder at him, she wore a smug smile. "Many of the residents of our little town would tell you it worked far too well."

"True," he laughed, lifting her off the rock and placing her on the ground. The way she was leaning over he had visions of fishing her out of the stream, her forehead bloody from hitting one of the jutting rocks at the edge. "Now be careful unless you're looking to go for a swim."

"I most certainly am not." She stepped back and her body was pressed against his again, not that he minded at all. In fact, he decided to live dangerously and wrapped his arms around her waist, effectively trapping her close. She felt and smelled better than anyone he'd ever known. "Thank you for bringing me out here today. I desperately needed time away from the house."

About that...

"I'm glad you're having a good time. But I have to admit that I feel terrible about leaving you last night. I barely slept, worrying about you and your sociopath of a neighbor. I already told Zach that since he had to leave today, I'm going to stay with you. I hope that's okay."

Not that it mattered if it wasn't. He wouldn't leave her un-protected either way but he was trying to be polite about it.

"Why did you feel badly? Zach was there."

Yes, he had been but Easton had not. He had to lie in bed imagining all the terrible things that could happen.

"And he's probably a hell of lot better at this protection thing than I am," Easton admitted. "I know he's done it for a living and all but I was really worried about you."

"And Leann."

Dizzy had Easton so turned around he barely remembered his own cousin. What was happening to him?

"Of course, that goes without saying. I just felt like I was abandoning you, going home to my safe house and leaving you there." He gave her a hopeful look. "I don't suppose I can talk you into staying at my place? Leann could stay with me or at Zach's place."

He had his own home in a nice neighborhood in Tremont about five miles from Dizzy, although he'd had the option to build on the ranch just like all the Andersons. He preferred to be closer to the office and town but he might be persuaded otherwise when he married and had a family.

She shook her head. "I need to keep an eye on Trip."

Easton wasn't going to give up so easily. This was Dizzy's life they were talking about.

"I can understand feeling that way before last night but now that we think he's buried the body, what are we watching for? He thinks he's covered his tracks and I'm guessing he'll go back to living his life as if nothing happened. He's going to want to act as normal as possible. At least that's what I would do."

Wrinkling her nose, Dizzy lowered herself onto the big rock and stretched out under the sun. "I'm not sure I like you identifying with a murderer."

"I'm not sure I like it myself but what options do I have?"

Easton settled next to her, the warm sun on his skin despite the cool temperatures, but by tonight it would be as cold as that stream. It was quiet for awhile, neither one saying anything but it wasn't uncomfortable or awkward. It was rare in his life when he didn't feel like he was "on" constantly.

"I've been pondering why I was the one to see this," Dizzy finally said after several minutes. "Why was I standing at that particular spot at just the right moment? Apparently none of the other neighbors were outside. Why did fate choose me? And this is not me boo-hooing as if I'm some sort of victim here. I'm not the victim, that poor girl is. What I'm wondering is why the universe wanted me to witness this. If I can figure that out, then

I think I can know what they want me to do about it. Or what I'm supposed to learn from this."

There it was. It had been hiding lately but Easton had always known it was there, although he wasn't annoyed by it like he thought he would be. In fact, he found himself wanting to help her figure it out.

"Maybe," he began cautiously. He didn't want her to be offended by his more logical approach to her problem, but he frankly wasn't a believer in all the mysticism. "Maybe you're not supposed to learn anything from this. Maybe it was just a coincidence. After all, most of your neighbors were probably watching television or on their phones, two activities you hate. If you think about it, it totally makes sense that you were the only one to witness it. Half of the people on your street don't even look out their windows once they're home from work. My street is the same way. I barely speak to my neighbors."

"True," she conceded with a nod, although her gaze was somewhere far away. She was thinking but she wasn't sharing it with him, probably because she thought he might make fun of it, "I had to make an effort to get to know the people in the cul de sac. I made them all gingerbread cookies at Christmas."

"I've baked nothing for my neighbors. But I try not to throw wild parties and run around naked."

Giggling, she slapped him lightly on the arm. "Nice of you. You said you try not to throw wild parties though. Does that mean that you do on occasion? Because I don't think I've ever received an invitation. I'm a little hurt about that."

Sadly, there were few – if any – of his friends he wanted to see without clothes. In fact, Dizzy was the one and only person on that list.

"I'll make sure to put you on the guest list for the next one. Seriously though, I don't think the universe is trying to send you a message."

Her brow arched and she gave him a wicked smile. "Perhaps you're the one being sent a message."

"That would be a waste. I'm a lost cause. But if they were, what message do you think the universe would send me? Read more? Get more sleep? I know, spend more time with your mother. Or maybe it would tell me to eat all of my vegetables. I'm terrible about that."

Those soft brown eyes were gazing at him again, but not with disdain or impatience. This time she liked what she saw and his own heart seemed to swell in his chest until he could barely breathe. Why had he never noticed just how beautiful Dizzy was? Or had it happened when he wasn't even looking? At this moment, just reclining on a rock wearing old blue jeans and a bright red sweatshirt, she was more gorgeous than any actress or model in a magazine.

"Maybe it would try and tell you that there's more out there than what you can physically experience."

His mouth had gone dry but he managed to get a few words out. "And I should open my mind?"

Her smile was gentle as was the chuckle that escaped those perfect lips. "I think perhaps you already have. You should give yourself more credit."

That he was growing as a human being? That would be a surprise.

"You're too kind to me. That might be the universe's message, you know. Stop being so easy on people. You're far too nice most of the time, even with people that don't deserve it."

"I am? How so?"

"You're polite when people are rude to you. Like the people at the art show or my so-called friends at the restaurant last night. They didn't deserve your patience or your kindness."

"You were patient too," she pointed out, stretching out her legs so that they dangled above the water. "But even if you or I had become angry and nasty, they wouldn't have really changed. No one can make another person modify their thoughts and behavior. I doubt anything you said to your friends is going to make them better or worse people. They are who they are."

Dizzy had a point but it still pissed Easton off that people could be so awful to one another. It was one thing for them to be closed-minded like himself; it was another to just be mean to anyone not like themselves.

"Is that your motto?" he teased. "You do you and I'll do me? The old live and let live?"

"Not a bad philosophy. I try not to judge others even if they judge me. Honestly, I don't have the time or inclination to go around sticking my nose in other people's business. It sounds exhausting."

"You don't want to judge me?" he asked. "Not even a little bit."

"Not even a little bit." She turned on her side, her head propped up on her palm. "And don't let anyone else do it either. You're just fine the way you are."

"Cold and calculating. Logical and reasonable. No flights of fancy here."

Reaching out she placed her hand on his. It was such a small gesture but from Dizzy it meant so much. "They couldn't say that today."

No, they certainly couldn't. And today was by far the best day he'd had in a long time. Because of her.

Now that is a flight of fancy.

Chapter Sixteen

EASTON HADN'T TRIED to kiss Dizzy when they were lying next to the stream but he should have. He'd been thinking about it but this whole relationship with her was so new. He wanted more with her but he didn't want to push. Taking a page from Dizzy's playbook, he was going to be fatalistic about it. If it was meant to happen…it would.

He couldn't will a relationship to happen – no matter how much he wanted it – and he couldn't make her feel romantic feelings about him. Last night she'd definitely acted like he was what she wanted and the same for this morning, but he also knew that for all Dizzy's talk about embracing life she was a cautious woman when it came to dating. She'd had a few boyfriends since returning to Tremont but not what he would call an active social life. While he had wholeheartedly cheered on her pickiness when it came to men before, now it was a different story.

So he'd thought about kissing Dizzy all through the ride back to Tremont and then during lunch as well. They'd stopped at the local diner to eat and practically every head in the place had swiveled to see the two of them walking in together. Apparently, the gossip mill was working overtime because no one looked surprised. They'd already heard about the date last night. He'd felt the weight of their gaze as they'd sat down and ordered and all through their meal. At one point, he'd thought Dizzy hadn't noticed but then she'd smiled behind her napkin when two older ladies walked by and practically tripped over their shoes because they'd been too busy staring to watch where they were going.

"We're like animals in the zoo," Easton muttered as the two women exited the diner. Unfortunately, there were still a couple of dozen people inside doing a terrible job of pretending that Easton and Dizzy weren't the center of attention and the topic of conversation.

Laughing, Dizzy took the last bite of chocolate cake. "Except they're stuck in cages and we can walk away any time. Does it really bother you that much?"

"Yes and no. Yes, because they're acting like us sitting in the same booth is such a shocking thing. No, because this town has the attention span of a gnat. They'll be on to the next thing in a few days."

"Well...I'm not the usual female that Easton Anderson dates."

She wasn't, thank goodness. She was so much more.

"I think that's a good thing."

He was rewarded with a smile. "You're such a sweet talker. Would you mind if we stopped into the bookstore for a minute? Elena said she found some interesting used books when she was in Seattle for the weekend and she wanted to show them to me."

He'd already paid the bill so he nodded and they stood up to leave, his hand on her lower back. Twenty-four sets of eyes followed their every movement until he and Dizzy were standing outside in the sunshine.

"I hope they find their new topic of gossip soon," he said as they walked two doors down to the bookstore. "You may be used to this but I'm not."

"After awhile you won't care, trust me."

He opened the door for her and it rang a bell to alert the proprietor. Elena's family had been running this bookstore for almost sixty years and everyone in town knew her and her mother and grandmother before her. At somewhere south of forty, she managed the store and her four children singlehandedly all while giving back to the community. She had donated stacks of books to the community center when it first opened and then on Christmas too so that every child would have a brand-new book from Santa.

The smiling woman waved at them from the top of a ladder where she was shelving books.

"Come on in. Are you here to look at those books, Dizzy?"

The smell of new and old books hit his olfactory senses and he couldn't stop the smile that immediately came to his face. There was something about a bookstore that made him happy.

"I am if this is a convenient time."

Elena scrambled down the ladder as if she was half her age. "Perfect timing. I was just going to take a break."

Easton nodded toward the back of the store where he knew she kept a large selection of historical biographies. "While you ladies do that, I think I'll go browse."

"There's a new Teddy Roosevelt back there you might want

to look at," Elena said. "Just came in the other day."

That was right up his alley so he made a beeline for the display, leaving Elena and Dizzy enthusiastically diving into a pile of musty old books behind the front counter. He was paging through the Teddy Roosevelt tome when he felt someone walk up behind him. Moving aside to let them peruse the bookshelf, he was shocked to see Madame Viola standing there looking incredibly normal. No bright colors or gold. No oversized earrings. If he didn't know better he would have taken her for a friendly grandmother picking out books for her grandchildren.

Clearing his throat, he nodded at the older woman. "It's nice to see you again, Madame Viola."

He felt a little silly calling her by her work name but he had no idea what her actual last name was. Or if Viola was even her real name.

She didn't greet him in return or even smile, her entire expression grave. "I'm glad I saw you. I've needed to speak to you."

Placing the book back on the shelf, he hoped this wasn't a complaint. Had the Accounts Payable department forgotten to cut her a check for the party? He went straight into businessman mode.

"Of course, how can I help you?"

She shook her head. "It's how I can help you. I received more messages and you need to know. Your soulmate is in danger. There is evil all around her."

"Um…yes, I remember you telling me that."

It wasn't information he was likely to forget even if he thought it was all bull.

"You have to protect her." Viola placed her hand on his arm, her tone urgent. "The evil is growing stronger."

By now the entire story about Dizzy, Trip, and the call to the police was all over town, of course, and clearly Madame Viola was exploiting it for her own gain. She'd made a lucky guess at the party last week but she was pushing this too far.

Straightening his shoulders, he tried to be as polite as possible but he wasn't going to take any crap either. This town needed to get their nose out of his life. He'd start with this woman.

"Madame Viola, I appreciate your concern but frankly this is none of your business, and I would ask that you leave me and also Dizzy Foster alone. I don't believe in psychics or mediums or any of that shit. I think you're taking a local gossip item and using it to your advantage, which I find reprehensible. Now if you will excuse me I need to leave."

Not waiting for a reply – because he didn't care what more she had to say – Easton strode back to the front of the store. Anger burned deep in his gut but he hadn't let it loose on Madame Viola as much as he could have. If the woman was smart, she'd give him a wide berth. In fact, the whole fucking town could do that as well. He was going to do what he wanted to do, say what he wanted to say, and date whomever he wanted to date.

Tremont could kiss his ass.

Chapter Seventeen

AFTER THE BOOKSTORE, Easton drove them to his home so he could pack an overnight bag. Dizzy had never been to Easton's home so she wasn't sure what to expect. She had a vision of ultramodern decor with lots of chrome and tile with all the rooms done in white, gray, or black. Sleek and clean and logical. Just the way he liked things. So she was speechless when he pushed open the front door and she stepped in.

Her first impression was warmth. Dark oak furniture in a Shaker style, leather furniture and large throw pillows in red, yellow, and blue. A couch she could sink into and never leave. Paintings on the walls–

Hold the phone. That was one of her paintings. Right there on the wall in between the living room and kitchen. Forgetting her tour of the home, she walked up to it, noticing that the homemade frame she'd put it in had been replaced by one that was worth far more than the actual picture. The wood gleamed and she couldn't stop herself from reaching out and running her finger down its smooth, cool surface.

"I had it re-framed about two years ago." Easton came to stand beside her. "It's one of my favorites."

She didn't paint many landscapes but she'd been in a phase and had painted part of the Anderson ranch and home. Like many of her paintings, she sold them on consignment at the local store or she donated them to a worthy cause. If she remembered correctly, she'd given this to one of the Anderson charities to be auctioned off for a new pediatric hospital ward.

Easton had to be reading her mind. "Yes, I bought it at auction. When I saw that it was the ranch, I had to have it. I outbid Shane and Noah. If Carter had been there I probably would have had to outbid him as well."

Easton had paid actual money for one of her paintings. She barely knew what to say.

"I never know where they end up. I never imagined you would have one."

"You have a great deal of talent, Dizzy."

His soft voice was right in her ear, his warm breath on her cheek. Dizzy could feel the heat from his body, standing so close to hers and she had a terrible impulse to reach out and run her hands down his chest.

Just to see if it felt as good as it looked.

Control yourself.

"Thank you."

A lump of emotion had risen in her throat that made it hard to speak. This logical, cold businessman had enough sentimentality to want a painting of his childhood home. It got her right in the feels. How was she supposed to stay even halfway detached when he acted like this? She was beginning to fall hard for this man of contradictions. She'd known him for years but she was beginning to believe that she'd never really known him at all.

"You're welcome. You want the nickel tour?"

She absolutely, positively did. If the living room was any indication she was in for more surprises. He led her into the kitchen which was a little more as she'd imagined, clean and modern. The appliances were stainless steel, the countertops granite, but there was still an air of home and comfort despite the more chilly furnishings. It might have been the bright red oven mitts on the counter next to the stove or perhaps the large copper frog by the sink that dispensed hand soap. It was nice to see he had a sense of whimsy.

"Nice," she commented. "Do you ever cook in here?"

"I do cook every now and then but I admit that it's not often enough. Does it look untouched by human hands? I'll tell the cleaning service they're doing a great job."

Dizzy inspected the refrigerator before answering. Spotless. "You should give them a raise too. I've never seen a stainless steel appliance not have fingerprints on it. At least one. It's amazing. Is there even food in there?"

Easton laughed and leaned against the counter. "Probably not much. Some sandwich meat, cheese, and a six pack of beer. The freezer has ice cream and frozen pizzas. I'm never without those. Ready to see the rest of the house?"

The rest of the home included Easton's office on the first floor and the master bedroom on the second floor. At the top of the stairs, he'd waved toward the end of the hall that there were two more bedrooms down there but that he hadn't really done anything with them.

Hesitating at the doorway of his room, Dizzy watched as Easton pulled a small duffel from the closet and began tossing clothing items into it. She would have pictured him packing with military precision and efficiency so it was amusing to see that this one activity was done rather haphazardly.

"I'll just be a second here," he said, disappearing into the ensuite bathroom before returning with a small leather toiletry case. "I think that's it. If I missed anything I guess I can always wear something of yours."

He was teasing about that, his blue eyes sparkling with mischief and his smile wide. For once with this man Dizzy wasn't going to hesitate. Instead, she walked right up in front of him and pulled his head down, crashing her lips against his.

The heat between them was instantaneous and before she could catch her breath Easton had her lying on top of his bed, his body hovering over hers as his mouth ravaged hers like a man thirsty after days in the desert. Blood rushed in her ears and the world tilted so she did the only thing she could to keep from falling. She grabbed Easton's shoulders and held on for dear life, hoping he could help her find steady ground even though he was the single reason she was reeling. Like a one-man wrecking crew, he'd smashed through all the reasons they shouldn't do this.

His lips trailed down her neck and nipped at the curve of her shoulder with his teeth, and then his tongue darted out immediately after to salve any wound he might have caused. Her fingers curled into his biceps and a strangled moan escaped her lips when he unerringly found that spot, right at the pulse point at the base of her neck, that made her crazy with want. If the rest of his instincts were that sharp this man was far more than an icy financier. He was temptation and she had no willpower.

But as quickly as it had begun it was over, a groan ripped

from somewhere deep in his chest as he dragged his lips away from hers. He rolled off of her and lay on his back on the mattress, his chest rising and falling rapidly. She didn't move either, afraid to ask the question that hovered on her tongue.

What did I do wrong?

Was it that little sister crap again? She was a grown woman and had been for some time now. She'd screwed up her courage enough to ask when he sat up on the bed, running his fingers through his tousled hair.

"I'm sorry about that. I kind of lost control there for a moment."

She'd never been one for pretense or games so it didn't occur to her to hide the truth.

"So did I."

Shaking his head, he leaned forward so his elbows were on his knees. Still not looking at her.

"It would be wrong of me to take advantage of your emotional state," he continued on as if she hadn't spoken. "You're in a vulnerable position with all that's happened and you don't need me to add to that by pressuring you...well, I just don't want to add to your problems or complicate the situation. I'm supposed to be helping you and keeping you safe, not ravishing you in my bedroom."

Sweet. Gallant. And entirely unneeded.

"You know I'm the one that started that, right? I kissed you."

He fidgeted and then stood up as if to put space between them. "You may have started it but I'm the one that pulled you down on the bed. I escalated things. I shouldn't have done that."

"Because I'm vulnerable?"

Scraping his fingers through his short dark hair – that appeared to be a habit when he was stressed – he made a snorting sound.

"I'm trying to be a gentleman here, Dizzy. You could help a man. Stopping was the last thing I wanted to do."

She gave him a mock surprised expression complete with wide eyes and open mouth. "Funny, that was the last thing I wanted to do too. Isn't that strange?" Then she stood and ran her fingers over his stubbly jaw. "But I do appreciate it. Not many men would have done that but then, you're not like every other guy."

"I'm definitely not as bright."

"That is true."

Reaching down, he pulled her to her feet and slid his arms around her waist. "This whole thing has just happened so fast and I–"

Pressing her fingers to his lips, she nodded in agreement. "It has but it's not like we're strangers. We've known each other almost our entire lives."

"These last few days I've felt like I never knew you at all and I'm sorry about that. I've made so many assumptions and even been one of those people who have called you strange or weird."

He didn't seem to understand that to her it wasn't an insult. "I am different and I'm glad about that. It's okay if others don't get it or me. I'm busy living my life. But it wasn't just you, actually. I made a few assumptions of my own."

He bent his head and brushed his lips over hers. "Let me guess. That I'm only wired for business and that I have little to no social skills?"

"Let's just say that I thought you took yourself a little too seriously, but now I know you have a wicked sense of humor."

He nodded solemnly. "I do. Did you hear the one about the horse who walked into a bar?"

"I have but that doesn't make it any less funny, so don't make such a long face."

They both cracked up and the tension hovering in the air completely dissolved away. Easton was her friend and, for now, her protector. He might just become more than that pretty quickly and that was fine too. This was nice. She'd never had a boyfriend that she'd been friends with before they were seeing each other. It certainly made things easier.

"I don't know too many jokes." He cleared his throat loudly. "That are clean enough to tell a lady anyway. I'll have to think of another one."

Dizzy beckoned to him as he picked up his duffel bag. "Stick with me, baby. I've got a million really bad jokes to tell you on the way back to my place. Let's start now. Knock, knock."

"Who's there?" he replied with a sigh, leading the way down the stairs.

Dizzy's mind was buzzing, formulating a plan. If any man in this world needed to loosen up and have some fun it was Easton. She'd start with jokes and then move on to music, maybe even some dancing. If he could do yoga, he could move to the beat.

Then she'd kiss him again and maybe this time they wouldn't stop.

Chapter Eighteen

Z ACH AND LEANNE were in Dizzy's living room when they arrived back at the house. Easton didn't even have a chance to ask Zach a question before the other man held out a manila folder.

"It's the preliminary background on Trip Stanford."

"Is that why you're back in town?" Easton asked, settling on the couch. "I thought you left on business."

Zach grinned. "I did leave and now I'm back. Turns out that particular bad guy walked into the sheriff's station and turned himself in. I'm officially unneeded on that assignment."

"I'm glad you're here and that you were able to get this."

"Anything to help us?" Dizzy asked as she sat next to Easton.

He opened the folder and they both began to page through the meager documents. Until about a week ago, it looked like Trip had lived a boring life. A mediocre student in both high school and college. Few extracurricular activities, although he'd played the saxophone in a jazz band in high school and was also a member of a science fiction club in college. He'd worked for a conglomerate in Seattle before moving to Tremont to be closer to family, where he'd taken a job in the marketing department of

Anderson Industries. Since then he'd been a model citizen except for one speeding ticket and a citation for parking in front of a fire hydrant.

His finances weren't anything out of the ordinary either. Trip, like many people, lived basically paycheck to paycheck with a mortgage he could barely afford, plus a hefty car payment on a pickup truck. He'd never been married and nothing in the charges on his credit card pointed to a current girlfriend.

All in all? A bust. Trip Stanford was a normal, everyday, run of the mill guy. Except that he wasn't really. He only appeared to be on paper. In real life, he was something far more sinister and deadly.

Easton looked up at Zach, who was hovering nearby. "Please tell me you're not done digging into this guy's past. There has to be more than this."

Dizzy looked as disappointed as Easton felt. "I appreciate the work you did, Zach. But I have to admit that I was hoping you'd find something in his past that would help us. I guess will have to find another way."

Leann came to sit next to her friend. "They're not stopping here. Jared is going to keep digging. They'll find something."

"This just means that this was probably his first time," Zach said. "He has no history of violence that we can find, so the good news is that the murder might not have been planned and that he's not looking to continue. The last thing we need in Tremont after the high school reunion is another spree killer."

Easton tightened his hold on Dizzy's hand. "Does that mean he's less dangerous or more? If he's never done this before he has to be scared and paranoid as hell. Then add in a witness neighbor and he has to be slowly losing his mind with worry and fear. When is he going to break and do something stupid?"

"So far he doesn't seem all that worried," Dizzy reminded him. "He walked over here the night he did it, cool as you please. As long as the town thinks I'm eccentric and not to be believed, he feels safe."

Zach smiled and nodded. "And that's exactly how we want him. Feeling comfortable and confident that he won't get caught. He's more likely to show his cards if he thinks nobody is looking at him. We just have to wait for him to make a mistake."

"What if he doesn't?" Easton asked. This entire situation was fucked up and there was little he could do about it. He hated that he couldn't fix this for Dizzy.

"Jesus, think positive," Zach replied grimly. "If he's a rookie he might have made more than one mistake. Maybe he held onto the woman's belongings. A lot of killers do as some sort of memento. It allows them to relive the moment over and over again. Or maybe he's afraid to throw her things in the trash until everyone – including Dizzy – has moved on. Burying her on his property wasn't the brightest idea so I don't think this guy is a criminal mastermind."

"He might have buried her things with her body in the backyard," Dizzy suggested. "That's what I would do. Get rid of it all at once. Of course, I wouldn't have chosen my own backyard."

Easton wouldn't have chosen that either but his cousin West was always reminding them that criminals weren't really all that smart or logical. If Trip had killed in a moment of high emotion, he wouldn't have had a plan in place.

"And that's why we're going to get him," Zach stated. "It

looks like he's kept all the evidence close by."

"But right now we have nothing," Dizzy said softly. "He might get away with this."

Leann pressed her lips together into a thin line. "We won't let him. We'll find a way."

"We will," Easton said, hoping he sounded as sure as Leann. "Stanford will end up behind bars."

But the question was how? The cops didn't believe them. They had no evidence, and no way to get any. Trip wasn't going to just walk into the police station and confess, like in Zach's case. Somehow he had to find a way to persuade the cops that Dizzy hadn't been drunk or dreaming when she'd witnessed the murder. They needed to find enough cause for the cops to search Trip's house a whole hell of a lot better than they had that first night. But how?

✦　✦　✦

DIZZY BREADED THE chicken cutlets and popped them into the pan to sauté, then gave the boiling pasta a stir. She was making chicken parmesan while Easton stood in the doorway of her back porch glowering at Trip Stanford's backyard, as if studying it for a long period would suddenly make everything clear and he'd know exactly what to do to put her neighbor behind bars.

If only it were that simple. She, too, had stared at that same place over and over but no lightning bolt of inspiration ever arrived, only a mounting frustration that Trip just might get away with it.

"It smells good in here."

He'd turned back to her although he'd left the door open,

the rapidly cooling air beginning to make the kitchen chilly. Rubbing the goosebumps on her arms, she wiped her hands on a paper towel and then walked around him to close the door.

"Thank you. It won't be long before dinner is ready. You could open the wine if you like. I'm afraid I don't have much of a selection. I'm more of a tequila girl when I drink."

Wincing, he must have realized he was cooling down the entire house. "Sorry, I was just–"

"Watching and looking," she finished for him. "I know. I do it too. I only closed the door because the temperature is dropping."

Easton shrugged awkwardly. "I don't know what I think I'm going to see. I just keep looking at that damn flowerbed…"

She retrieved a small spoon from the utensil drawer and dipped it into the sauce. "I know how you feel. I can't help it either. Here, take a taste of the sauce and tell me what it needs."

She loved the way Easton's eyes closed with pleasure as his lips wrapped around the spoon. Then he made a yummy sound that was music to her ears.

"Honey, that's amazing. I don't think it needs anything."

Laughing, she reached for the salt and pepper. "I've barely seasoned it. It has to need something."

"Seriously, it's fine the way it is."

Her hand hovered over the simmering sauce and she finally sighed and put down the shakers. "Okay, I'll leave it the way it is. Are you hungry?"

"Starving," he declared, opening the refrigerator and reaching for a bottle of wine. "Where's your opener?"

With her free hand that wasn't turning the cutlets, she fished out the corkscrew that was hiding under a ladle and a cheese grater. It only took him moments to open the wine and pour two glasses, placing them on the dinner table. This was a dinner for two as Leann and Zach had gone out to dinner and a movie. Leann had made a big production – wink wink, nudge nudge – about how they wouldn't be home before eleven-thirty.

Easton's phone buzzed in his pocket for about the dozenth time in the last hour. He glanced at it but simply tucked it back in his shirt, not bothering to answer.

"Someone really wants to talk to you. Maybe you should answer it."

"It's not just one person, although most of the calls are from my second in command. They're panicking because I'm not there but so far nothing has come up that can't wait until tomorrow. Today has made me realize that I've been doing my staff a great disservice by never taking any time off. They're smart and capable but I haven't given them the opportunity to shine all on their own. Would you like me to set the table?"

He could help her in the kitchen anytime. Was there anything sexier than a man with his sleeves rolled up helping do mundane domestic chores?

"Yes, thank you. Dishes are in that cupboard to my right." She placed the cutlets on a platter and laid cheese on top before slipping them into the oven. It would only take a minute or two for the cheese to melt and the oven was already hot from the garlic bread. "I think it's nice that you're giving your staff more responsibility. But it is probably scary for them."

She reached for the large pot of boiling pasta but Easton's hands were there first. Standing behind her, his body close to her, she was reminded of how handsome and sexy he was, and how sweet and helpful. When he wanted to be.

"Let me get this for you. It's heavy."

He gently nudged her out of the way and drained the noodles in the colander in the sink, steam billowing in the air along with the tempting aroma of tomatoes and garlic. She quickly filled their plates and they settled at the table, but there was an unspoken tension between them. She could practically feel Easton's frustration and unhappiness as if it were a tangible item she could touch and see. By the end of the meal, she couldn't take the silence any more. Men might not talk about their feelings but maybe with some encouragement this one would.

"Do you want to talk about it?"

His fork paused halfway to his mouth. "It?"

"Yes, it. Whatever *it* is that's pissing you off. I'm assuming it's not me this time. Or is it?"

Placing his fork on the edge of his plate, he wiped his hands on the napkin. "It's not you. It's just…"

Dizzy didn't say anything, simply waiting while he put his thoughts together. Pushing him wasn't the way to go. It never was with an Anderson.

"I can't fix this for you," he said after a long pause, a muscle ticking in his jaw. "I'm not a cop like West or an ex-DEA agent like Jason or even a former bodyguard and soldier like Zach. I'm a guy who sits at a desk most of the time and that's not what you need right now. I'm useless to you."

He really believed it too. Easton was one of the smartest men she knew, possibly the smartest, and he thought he was useless. Time to set him straight.

She looked around the kitchen, twisting first left and then right in her chair for effect. "Funny, I don't see anyone else here keeping me safe. I must have missed them. Are they upstairs taking a nap?"

"Any guy could do this."

Standing, she pushed her chair back and then walked to the front door, opening it and checking outside. "I don't see any of those men lining up to do the job. Looks like you're the only one willing."

"Very funny. I'm being serious here."

She didn't take her chair again, instead moving behind him and dropping a kiss on his cheek while her hands rested on his wide shoulders. Shoulders that had taken on the responsibility of this situation. He thought he had to solve this all by himself, but they were in this together.

"So am I. It is not your job to fix all the little and big problems in my life. I'm a grown woman and I have to deal with this on my own. But I am glad that I have friends to help me because doing this alone would be difficult, if not impossible. Let me say this again in case I wasn't clear...none of this is your responsibility and I'm grateful for all that you've done up to now. Technically if you hadn't given Leann a ride here that night you wouldn't be involved at all."

He didn't turn to look at her, his gaze still directed toward his plate. "Is that what I am? A friend?"

There was so much vulnerability in that simple question. And so much that he hadn't asked.

Out loud.

It was up to her to answer. She could tell him he was only a friend but that wouldn't be the truth. And one thing Dizzy felt strongly about was telling the truth even when it was hard or scary. Saying it terrified her. Their relationship had changed so much in the last week and she'd seen a side of Easton that she'd been unsure even existed. He was a friend but that wasn't the end of it. He could be her lover...and maybe more. Did this relationship have staying power? Was he even in it for the long haul or for a few nights of pleasure? He'd never shown an interest in settling down.

And neither have I, until now. Is that what I want? With him?

Mustering all her courage, she ran her hands down his arms so their fingers were entwined and her chin was resting on his shoulder.

"You are so much more to me than a friend, although I'm not sure I have the words to express what you are in my life. I just know that I want you here with me."

Easton wasn't the flowery words type so she wasn't sure how he would even respond. There was a small beat of silence and then his fingers tightened around her own.

"Good, because that's where I want to be."

For him, that was high praise indeed.

Chapter Nineteen

ASTON HAD BEEN shooed out of the kitchen when it was time to do the dishes with some lame excuse that he was a guest so he didn't have to help with housework. He'd made the counterargument that she'd done most of the cooking but one look at Dizzy's cute but stubborn little chin and he'd clearly seen he wasn't going to win. Instead, she'd ask him to light a fire in the fireplace as the temperature was dropping quickly.

Stepping out onto the back porch to get an armload of wood, Easton stopped and stared at Stanford's house. His gaze automatically went to that window where Dizzy had watched her neighbor strangle an unknown woman.

An unknown woman.

But she had to be known to someone. Surely family or friends had to be wondering where she was.

Scooping up the firewood, he strode back into the kitchen where Dizzy was loading plates into the dishwasher.

"I think we need to take a different route. If looking at Trip doesn't get us anywhere maybe we should look at his victim."

Dizzy dried her hands on a dishtowel and seemed to weigh his words. "But we don't know who she is."

"Somebody does and they miss her. Chances are she has friends and family, at least one if not the other. They might have filed a missing persons report when she disappeared and they couldn't get in touch with her."

Dizzy smiled, renewed hope in her eyes. "That's brilliant. We'll get going on that tomorrow. Someone, somewhere has to be wondering where she is and what's happened to her. You're pretty brilliant, Easton Anderson."

He didn't feel brilliant. It felt like he was finally making a contribution.

"I think you're giving me far too much credit but thank you. Now I better get that fire started, it's freezing out there."

It didn't take long to get the fire going as he'd done it a time or two hundred. He settled onto the floor next to the fireplace and stretched out his legs as he settled back onto an oversized cushion that he knew Dizzy had made with her own two hands. Splashed with color, it was like everything else in this room – comfortable and bright. A little like being with Dizzy. She made his usually gray world technicolor.

It wasn't that he was unhappy or depressed. That wasn't it at all. But his life had fallen into a pattern these last few years. Work had become the be-all and end-all of his existence and like most things that he'd done for a long time, the newness has worn off. There was rarely a surprise, even when there were problems and issues to battle. There was hardly any challenge and it all felt a little too easy recently as if he'd done it all before and he was caught in the movie *Groundhog Day*.

But with Dizzy, everything felt like the first time. It was the way she looked at life, so different from his own perspective. She had an artist's eye and to her even the most mundane detail took on a completely different meaning.

"I hope you're still hungry."

Pulled from his thoughts, he saw Dizzy standing in front of him with an armload of food and a triumphant smile.

"I'm pretty sure I see marshmallows. If you're thinking s'mores you might be the most perfect woman on earth."

Dropping to her knees on the soft rug she dumped the food on the coffee table next to them. "Being perfect sounds awful. Who would want to be that? Everyone knows it's the imperfections that make something or someone interesting."

Easton was beginning to believe that. He only hoped it worked in reverse too. Did Dizzy find his flaws fascinating or frustrating? In his experience, the women he'd dated all wanted to change him. Some in small ways and others wanted to completely make him over, but he'd never quite been good enough just the way he was.

Dizzy had indeed brought the fixings for s'mores and she quickly slapped chocolate onto graham cracker squares while Easton slipped marshmallows onto long skewers. Handing one skewer to her, he held his up high over the warm flames, hating when they got too burnt. Dizzy, on the other hand, shoved hers right into the flames and then had to pull it out, blowing and giggling as she tried to extinguish the fire.

Christ on a unicycle, they even roasted marshmallows the same way they lived. Him? Cautious and thoughtful. Dizzy? Full speed ahead and worry about the problems later. He could only wonder if everyone was like this. He made a mental note to check at the next Anderson bonfire.

They smashed their marshmallows between the graham crackers and chocolate before taking a greedy bite. Eating a s'more was never an elegant or delicate activity. Dizzy had a dollop of chocolate at the corner of her mouth and he had a sudden urge to lean forward and lick it away, then head south to parts even more interesting.

Never before had eating dessert been so...arousing. His palms were sweating, his heart racing, and his pants uncomfortably tight. It was like being a teenager all over again and he'd hated those adolescent years. Here he was, a grown man ten years Dizzy's senior, and he didn't know whether to kiss her or act like none of this affected him in the least.

Their gazes locked and the room suddenly went from cozy to sauna-like in seconds, the fire way too hot. Her amber-colored eyes were dark with...desire? At some point their bodies had swayed closer until she was so near he could smell the delicate scent of her skin, creamy and soft and begging to be touched. Very slowly, so as not to break the spell, he gently wiped away the chocolate on her lip with his thumb, giving her ample time to move away before bringing it to his own mouth. The sweetness burst on his tongue and made him want to beg for more.

"Easton."

His name was a sigh on her lips and he wanted to hear her say it over and over while he was deep inside of her, driving them both to ecstasy. He wanted to be as close to her as two people could possibly be. His mind blanked and his world narrowed to only this woman. The primitive feelings only she evoked him in were battering at the cages that his civilized mind kept them in, safely locked away where he could pretend they didn't exist. But he could no longer deny that he wanted Dizzy with a ferocity that he couldn't keep locked away anymore. With only one look, she had to know what he was thinking and feeling.

The distance between them was a nuisance that they didn't need. He hesitated, their lips mere millimeters from meeting, not wanting to assume anything. Suddenly he didn't have to. Dizzy had leaned in and brushed her mouth over his so softly it could have been the wings of a butterfly fluttering against his flesh. Deepening the kiss, he ran his tongue over her lower lip until she opened to him.

Dessert cast aside, he situated her underneath him as they both stretched out in front of the fireplace. Orange and gold flames danced in the dim light casting shadows on the walls as if to exhort and encourage. He didn't need a cheering section as he propped himself up on his elbows, not wanting to crush Dizzy. He captured her soft chocolate-covered lips in another sizzling kiss as he lowered one hand down the side of her body, his fingers tracing the enticing curves of her body. First to her generous breast, the nipple hard beneath his palm, before lingering at the indentation of her waist, then on to where her hips flared and the gentle swell of her perfect bottom began.

Trailing kisses over her delicate jaw, he paused to give her earlobe a nip and then traveled down her throat to the open neckline of her blouse. Nosing it aside, he revealed the lacy edge of her bra and he couldn't stop himself from tracing it with his tongue. He could feel her shudder and shake against him, and his own heart beat in time with hers as if they'd somehow melded together into one being.

He didn't consciously begin undressing her but somehow her

blouse and jeans melted away, leaving her in her bra and panties. He had expected white and utilitarian undies but of course, Dizzy never stopped surprising him. What he saw took what was left of his breath away, making him want to fall to his knees in pure worship. She was a goddess and he a willing supplicant.

Lace. Satin. A pretty lavender with ecru edging. Her breasts spilled out of the cups just covering the pink nipples that had hardened under his gaze. Strumming them softly with his thumbs, they tightened further and Dizzy began moving restlessly against him, her thigh brushing his painfully hard cock.

So far, she'd been as eager and wanting as he was but he needed to be sure. Their relationship was still so new and this was a giant step forward. Once they became lovers, they couldn't go back to being friends.

Brushing a stray strand of her long dark hair from her face, he lightly caressed her shell-like ear. "Are you sure?"

Holding his breath, he waited for the answer. If she said no, he'd be fine with that. Crushed and disappointed, of course, but he'd live. Probably. He couldn't be too sure. He only knew that he'd never wanted a woman to say yes so badly in his entire life, and that included his first time with Amy Betts back in high school when he'd been sure that a man could die from a case of blue balls.

His doubts, however, were dashed away when Dizzy smiled and her own fingers reached up to trace his lips. Just that soft touch had him riding the edge. It wasn't going to take much to send him over and he was a grown man, not a teenager. That's how crazy she made him.

"I'm sure."

Chapter Twenty

NOT FOR A moment had Dizzy thought to say no. She wanted to make love with Easton and she wasn't ashamed in the least to admit it. Despite her rather open upbringing, Dizzy wasn't casual about sex. Tami and Louis had taught her that there was nothing shameful about sex and they'd encouraged her to explore her urges during those tumultuous teen years and then in college, although less since they were thousands of miles apart. If Dizzy had brought home a boyfriend they wouldn't have blinked an eye if he'd slept in her room.

But maybe because her parents hadn't made sex so taboo, Dizzy hadn't felt the need to run around and try every guy she dated. Frankly, she was persnickety about who she took off her clothes for and lately she hadn't slept with anyone. She simply hadn't met a man that made her want to have sex in the last year. Until Easton.

Her eager fingers fumbled with the buttons on his shirt but managed to free them despite her haste. Easton shrugged off the offending garment and tossed it away so that his torso was bared for her viewing – and touching – pleasure. Easton still pitched in around the ranch and it showed in every hard line of his body.

Trailing her fingers down the center of his chest, she traced every ridge and plane of his flat abdomen, the skin warm under her questing fingers, delighting in the moans she was able to elicit from his lips.

She must not have been moving fast enough, however, because he was tugging at the buckle of his belt and then unfastening his trousers, the sound of the zipper sliding down loud in the room. Kicking his pants away, he stripped off his socks and boxers at the same time, leaving him naked as the day he was born.

Dizzy couldn't help but look. And perhaps she stared a little too long because she heard Easton chuckle as he sat back on his haunches. "Like what you see?"

Hell, yes.

His skin was golden, his body sculpted from the finest of marble, and…

He was gloriously aroused as well, and it was she that made him that way. Currently he was looking her up and down like he wanted to eat her up. She'd be just fine with that, but first she needed to touch him.

"Baby," he breathed when her hands glided down his chest and over his belly. Her fingers encircled him, hot, hard, and ready, sliding up and down until he groaned, his hand covering hers to stay her movements. "I'm on the edge here."

"Wouldn't it be terrible if we had to start all over again?" she teased, her fingers slipping down to caress the base and then even farther to his balls, already drawn up tight. "I wouldn't mind."

His blue eyes were dark with desire, his pupils blown wide with arousal. His expression was almost feral and her own pulse hitched higher as she saw her own emotions reflected in his gaze.

"There are things I want to do to you first, Desiree. But we need to have that awkward conversation. I'm clean and healthy. What about you?"

"Just had my annual a few months ago and I'm good. I'm on the pill too."

It was sweet that he had stopped to take care of business. He leaned down to kiss her again, all too brief but very sweet. "Even your name is about desire. I never even noticed before. Desiree."

She'd always hated her real first name but the way it tripped off of his tongue she almost found it palatable.

Reaching behind her, Easton efficiently unclipped her bra and then drew it down her arms before tossing it away. Her panties quickly followed and now they were both bare, skin to skin as he pressed himself close. His tongue played with the hard tips of her breasts and then sucked them into his mouth, giving them a gentle tug with his teeth that sent arrows of pleasure straight to her clit as if they were directly connected. The blood roared in her ears and quicksilver flew through her veins as he lavished attention on her breasts, even running his tongue on the sensitive flesh along the underside. Not one inch of skin was left untouched when he finally gave her a moment to catch her breath.

She drew precious oxygen into her starving lungs as his lips now traveled down over her soft abdomen to her already drenched slit. The room tilted and spun as his tongue delved into her folds, seeking and exploring but never settling into any rhythm. He held her there on the edge, his tongue and then his fingers dancing around her already swollen and achy clit.

Pressing first one and then a second finger inside her, he unerringly found that special spot that other men seemed to ignore. With his digits rubbing her from the inside and his thumb drawing circles around her sensitive button there was only one sure result and it came quickly. When her orgasm hit, her body bowed off the floor as white-hot heat suffused every cell. She rode the waves of her star-spangled climax until she lay spent and satisfied, her body covered in a sheen of sweat.

Lifting her heavy lids, Dizzy found Easton kneeling between her legs and tearing open a foil packet with his teeth. In a short moment he was there, nudging at her slick entrance as his lips found a sensitive spot right under her ear. Her fingers dug into the muscles of his shoulders as he pressed forward, filling and stretching her walls. It had been awhile and for a moment there was a twinge of pain, but he must have sensed it and immediately stopped until she lifted her hips and urged him on again.

She couldn't remember ever feeling this full but then Easton had successfully wiped out any and all memories of other men, and he'd done it with little effort. Slowly he pulled out almost all of the way before snapping his hips and driving back into her. Sweet pleasure dripped through her veins and pooled in her belly. Over and over he repeated the movements as his mouth explored her neck and shoulders. She'd have love bites to cover tomorrow.

But Easton would have a few marks of his own. Her nails dug into the flesh of his back as he pistoned in and out of her, her legs wrapped around his lean waist. The only sound in the room were their ragged breaths and the sound of skin on skin. A bar of arousal was building in her abdomen and flames licked along her flesh. It felt like her entire body might spontaneously combust.

Each stroke sent her higher until she broke apart into a million tiny pieces, like shards of glass floating in the air and spinning around the room in a kaleidoscope of color and light. Easton reached his peak right after and she gazed at him, fascinated as emotions flitted across his tortured features. First pain, then pleasure, and finally pure male satisfaction.

They collapsed together, a sweaty tangle of arms and legs, as Dizzy tried to get her heart and breathing under control. Somehow he'd maneuvered them so he was lying on his back and she was tucked into his side. She stroked his damp chest and pressed baby kisses everywhere she could reach. His heart pumped beneath her fingers and she could feel it as slowed into a regular rhythm.

Neither one of them wanted to break the comfortable silence but she knew it would be Easton who would speak first. He wasn't a man that enjoyed quiet, although she could tell he was becoming more appreciative of it.

"That was…"

Giggling, she nodded her head in the dim light. "Yes, it was."

He didn't need to find the right words because they probably didn't exist. Fantastic and amazing just weren't cutting it. It was…transcendent.

"You didn't like…cast a spell or something over us, did you? Because that's better than anything I've ever experienced, so it would make sense if there were some witchcraft involved here."

Levering up on her elbow, she gave his arm a light slap. "For the last and final time, I am not a witch. I don't cast spells. I don't know the future. And I can't read minds. I'm simply an empathetic person who believes in the creative soul. That's a completely different thing."

His smile widened as his fingers trailed down her back to land on her bottom, giving it a playful squeeze. "Are you sure you can't read minds? I bet you can tell me what I'm thinking about right now."

Gulping, her eyes widened in surprise. "Again? Already?"

Easton was apparently going to give her as much as she could handle and then some.

"I told you, it's like someone has cast a spell over me. I'm like a teenager again."

She was feeling the effects of that spell as well. Could it be…love?

✦   ✦   ✦

EASTON WAS HAVING the most amazing dream ever. He was floating on a cloud in a bluer than blue sky while Dizzy pleasured him with her mouth. His hands were fisted in the soft fluff of the cloud and his limbs were heavy and languorous as her soft, wet tongue flitted up and down his aching shaft. He should have dreams like this more often. It was so fucking real.

Groaning as the warm cavern of her mouth engulfed the head, his hips bucked as he pressed himself in farther. With a jolt of awareness, his eyes snapped open and he realized the fluffy cloud he'd been gripping was Dizzy's long, silky hair and that her mouth was indeed working magic. As much as he loved her oral skills, he preferred to be buried deep inside of her so they could both get there at the same time.

The sun was beginning to filter through the curtains, which told him that it was morning and they'd soon have to get out bed and go to work. Because that's what grownups did. Right now, though, he was still in teenage boy mode, and that guy was horny as hell. Easton's dick was doing all the thinking at the moment.

"Baby," he breathed, extricating his fingers from her tresses. "Get up here and ride me."

With a coquettish smile she did just that, swinging a leg over his body so that she was straddling his thighs. She must have read the urgency in his tone because she didn't play games, tease, or make him wait, instead sinking down on him until he was in to the hilt. Hot, wet, and tight. Being inside of Dizzy was the closest thing to nirvana that he'd ever experienced.

A sigh of pleasure came from her full, swollen lips and she swiveled her hips as she pulled up and then slammed back down, drawing an answering moan from his throat. The little witch had him exactly where she wanted him, helpless but happy. He was already thinking of reasons to call in sick today so they could stay and bed and continue making love all day long.

Like a cowgirl on a wild bull, she rode him fast and hard, their breathing coming in gasps and sweat trickling down their torsos. Her long dark hair hung in a curtain over her body, playing a game of peek a boo with her breasts. His hands found the pink tips, pinching them until they were rock hard and she was arching her back in pleasure.

His name fell from her lips like a prayer as they drove closer to that shimmering destination. Balls pulled up tight, the pressure in his lower back began to grow and his hand slid down her body to find her clit with his thumb, pressing and rubbing in circles.

Her channel clamped down on him as her orgasm hit her, setting off his own completion. His fingers flexed on her hips as he held her in place, his muscles rigid and his frame stiff. She fell against his chest when they were finished, her cheek over his heart. Not wanting to ever move, he stroked her back and hair, content to lie there with her all day if she wanted to. He'd never felt this close to a woman in his entire life, but then sex with Dizzy would never be mundane or boring. He should have known that. This was a woman that took everything she did from the ordinary and made it into a work of art.

So he was disappointed when she eventually began to stir, sliding off of him with a quick kiss to the lips.

"You have to go to work today."

"Don't want to. I'm the goddamn boss. They can't fire me."

Giggling, she laid on her side and ran a fingertip across his jaw, rough with a night's stubble. "No, they can't but they need you."

"They can do without me. In fact, I'm thinking of retiring young. Work is overrated."

Dizzy sat up, her cheeks pink with mirth. "Who is this man in my bed and what have you done with Easton Anderson? He's a workaholic, so I know you're an imposter."

"It's a spell," he complained, throwing an arm over his eyes. The sun's rays were coming into the room stronger than before. It was getting late. "You're a witch and you've got me under a spell. I'm helpless against you. There ought to be laws or something. I've lost the will to work."

"You'll get it back once you're in your office. Then you'll remember that you're a captain of industry. A fierce, tiger-like CEO." She reached across him and retrieved his cellphone from the nightstand. "I bet you have dozens of emails that only you can deal with."

She was probably right, but if he started looking at his phone then he'd be sucked into that world.

"You can't make me go to work."

"That's true. You could spend the day with me, I suppose. I have to go to the post office, then the community center. I also need to stop at the grocery store and the dry cleaners."

He didn't want to do that either.

"You won't stay in bed with me all day?"

"I can't," she said with a smile, shaking her head. "But if you work hard at the office today I'll make sure that you're well rewarded tonight."

It was probably the best deal he was going to get.

"Fine, I'll go to work. But I still think I've been placed me under a spell."

It was either that or he'd fallen hopelessly in love. He wasn't sure which was more frightening.

Chapter Twenty-One

IT WAS A gorgeous morning and it didn't have anything to do with Dizzy's night with Easton. Not at all. It was simply the weather, cool and crisp.

And the amazing night she'd had with Easton. There. She'd admitted it. Now she was beginning to understand why Leann was always in such a great mood, happy, smiling, and humming. Dizzy wasn't a person who hummed as she went about her errands but today she was doing it, and it was all Easton's fault. At this rate, she'd be singing arias in the frozen food section of her local supermarket.

Which was where she was now, standing in the baking aisle picking out chocolate chips. She'd grabbed a bag of semi-sweet but she was thinking she might want bags of dark and white chocolate as well. She'd already thrown brown sugar and flour into her cart along with a pound of butter from the dairy aisle. Easton had a sweet tooth and she was planning to make him chocolate chip cookies this afternoon while he was at the office. All she needed was a couple of steaks and she'd be set. Turning to head to the back of the store, Dizzy froze as her cart almost bumped into someone standing directly in her path.

Trip Stanford.

Why isn't he at work? It's too early for lunchtime. And why is he smiling at me? It's creepy.

"Dizzy, I didn't expect to see you here." He peered into her cart while she tried not to let her shock and horror show. He was the last person she wanted to be around or talk to. "Looks like you're baking again. You definitely have a reputation as one of Tremont's finest cooks."

What do I say to a killer when he compliments me?

"Yes, I am planning to bake today," she finally managed to say, proud of herself that she sounded almost normal, although she was sure her face was white as a sheet.

"Cookies or cake?" he asked, still surveying the contents of her cart. "When the weather is nice and the windows are open I can sometimes smell your cookies all the way to my house."

"Cookies," she croaked, her calm veneer beginning to crack. The longer she was standing next to him the worse it was. The images from that terrible night came rushing back, crowding out normal thought processes. All she knew was that this man had killed a woman with his bare hands. Then he'd acted like nothing had happened.

Straightening, Trip smiled but to Dizzy it looked slimy and contrived. Not natural and easy. "Delicious. I think my favorite dish you make is pot roast though. You made it the other night, didn't you? With carrots, potatoes, and homemade dinner rolls."

She had but how did he know? He couldn't have smelled it because she didn't have the windows open that night.

Unless he'd been watching her. Looking in the windows? Was he so confident now that he was *taunting* her? What an asshole.

A shudder ran through her and her fingers tightened on the handle of the cart until her knuckles were white. She was determined that this murderer wouldn't see any visible reaction to his words.

"I make it quite a bit. It's an easy dish."

"Dizzy? There you are. I thought I'd lost you. Are you ready to go?"

Easton's younger brother Carter was suddenly standing next to her, and Dizzy couldn't imagine being happier to see anyone than she was right now at this very moment. Taking a calming breath, she forced a smile to her face.

"I think we got separated in the produce section but I'm glad you found me. And yes, I am ready to go."

Somehow Carter had insinuated himself between Trip and Dizzy. She could almost breathe normally with him standing there.

"Excuse us," Carter said to Trip, not waiting for any acknowledgement. He simply commandeered Dizzy's cart and started pushing it in the opposite direction while keeping a casual hand on her shoulder. They were in line at the cashier when he finally spoke again. "Are you okay?"

"I am now," she replied, palpable relief running through her veins. She hadn't realized how tense she was until she wasn't anymore. "Thank you, by the way. He was trying to engage me in conversation. Why, I don't know."

They didn't speak anymore as Dizzy's groceries were rung up and then Carter helped her load the bags into the back of her car.

"If you don't mind I'll follow you back to your place."

She didn't mind in the least, although the trip was only a mile and a half. They were pulling up in her driveway in less than three minutes. Carter offered to help her unload her haul and she accepted gratefully. Honestly, she didn't want to be by herself. She'd thought it would be okay in the daylight when Trip was at work but she wasn't too proud to admit the encounter had shaken her.

When she'd put the last of her groceries away, she still wasn't quite ready to be alone yet.

"How about a cup of coffee?"

"I wouldn't say no." Carter sat down at her table and she bustled around the kitchen, starting another pot and placing some cookies on a plate. These were a batch of oatmeal she'd made three days ago and there weren't many left after Easton had found them in the pantry. "How long had you been talking to Trip when I walked up?"

Sighing, she sank into the chair opposite, propping her chin up with her hand. "Not long. A few minutes. It was so creepy. I was picking out chocolate chips and then I turned around and there he was. Just like in one of my nightmares."

"What did he want?"

"That I don't know. He made a comment about my baking smelling so good when the windows are open. Oh, and this was weird…he mentioned that he liked the smell of the pot roast I made the other night, but I didn't have the windows open. So how did he know? Is he watching me?"

Carter's jaw was tight and she'd bet anything that his teeth were gritted together. She'd seen Easton do the same thing when he was pissed off.

"He might be. It sounds like he's trying to intimidate you, Dizzy."

"Why?" she asked. It didn't make any sense. "Everyone believes him and no one believes me."

"We believe you, and I bet he knows it. He may be confident right now but there has to be a part of him that's sweating inside. Even if he thinks you'll let it go and give up he has to know that the Andersons won't."

Standing, she poured two cups of coffee and added cream and sugar to hers but Carter took his black. She'd made it enough times at Sunday dinner to know. Easton took his with one sugar, no cream.

"For someone who's scared he doesn't act it. He seems pretty sure of himself. It's like he knows he's got off scot free."

Carter shook his head. "He's scared. Trust me, he's shaking in his boots. That's why he's keeping tabs on you. This is far from over and he knows it. Right now, it's all about intimidation. Seeing if he can get you to drop the whole thing and change your story. He might not have acted frightened when he talked to you, but he was definitely pale when I showed up."

"Can I say thank you again?" Dizzy sighed, sipping her coffee. "I don't know what I would have done if you hadn't been there."

Chuckling, Carter helped himself to a cookie. "You'd be just fine. You're an honorary Anderson, after all."

That was sweet but she wasn't sure it was true. She also doubted Tami and Louis would be happy hearing that news.

"I wonder why he was in the grocery store in the middle of

the day. Shouldn't he be at work?" Another thought occurred to her. "Wait…shouldn't you be at work too?"

Popping the last bite of cookie into his mouth, Carter nodded. "Technically, I am at work. I was just meeting with the owner of the store discussing some of the renovations they're planning in the next few months. That's when I saw you looking like you'd rather be having a root canal than talking to that bastard. As for Stanford, maybe he took a vacation day. He's probably exhausted from hiding what a monster he is."

"Just when I think this can't get any more strange I'm proven wrong. If I were Trip I'm the last person I'd be talking to."

If that sentence made any sense at all.

"That's because you're a nice person who wouldn't hurt a fly." Carter grinned as he stood, pushing back his chair. "Although if you want to give Easton a punch in the nose when he's acting like an ass you'll have me in your cheering section. Don't let him push you around, Dizzy, or make you think you need to change who you are to be with him."

"He hasn't made me feel that way at all," Dizzy vowed, making a cross-your-heart motion with her fingers. "He's been great, actually. I'm seeing a whole new side to him. But I still wouldn't punch him. You know that the Foster family are strictly pacifists."

"You just say the word and I'll do it," Carter offered. "Now I better get back to the office or they'll send out a search party for me. Seriously, Dizzy, call me if you need anything. Day or night. We're here for you no matter what you need."

She stood as well and gave him a big hug. "Thank you, Carter. The way your family has stood behind me these last several days has meant the world to me."

"There was never a question that we'd do anything else."

Buoyed by his certainty, Dizzy walked Carter to his truck and waved goodbye as he drove away. She'd been brought up not to care what people thought about her, but it did feel good to know that she had friends on her side. This was one of the big reasons she'd moved back to Tremont. She had good, loyal friends here, and she needed all the help she could get to find a way to prove what she saw that night.

Chapter Twenty-Two

E ASTON FLIPPED OPEN the folder on his desk, scanning the contents. Trip Stanford's original resume he'd sent in before being hired. Copies of his annual performance reviews. Salary and bonus history. Deciding he might as well start at the beginning, Easton picked up the resume for a closer look.

Stanford had attended a university on the West Coast and studied business. Easton already knew that Trip had received mediocre grades and didn't have much in the way of extracurriculars. His one item of note on the resume was that he'd done an internship with a Wall Street firm for two summers.

Flipping over the resume, Easton read through the scrawled and cryptic notes on the backside that the interviewer had made. It was company policy to make notes on the resume if possible. Sadly, the recruiter had only done the bare minimum.

Wall Street internship.

Smiling. Friendly. Makes eye contact.

Understands marketing principles.

Good problem solving.

Eager to work.

Seems ambitious.

Easton made a mental note to talk to Leann about updating the Human Resources procedures regarding recruiting and interviewing. This wasn't much to go on and was vague at best. All he could get from this was that Trip had smiled and made a good impression and hadn't blown any of the situational questions that he'd been asked. Is that all it took to be hired by Anderson Industries? He needed to talk to Shane and Travis and take a look at hiring standards as well. Maybe they needed to do some sort of psychological exam.

Which reminded him that anyone that worked for Anderson had to have a criminal background check done before hiring. Where was Stanford's? Easton already knew what it would say courtesy of Jason's colleague Jared but it should be in the file.

"Amy," he barked out to his assistant just outside the door. Thank goodness she was used to him and the way he worked. He'd gone through about a dozen assistants before she took the job. Sometimes he wondered whether he worked for her rather than the other way around. She was priceless and she didn't take any of his shit. Kind of like Dizzy, only with no discernible talent for painting. "Is this the whole file?"

Amy hurried into his office, dressed in a navy blue suit and low-heeled shoes. "Stop bellowing, for heaven's sake. They could probably hear you down in the cafeteria. Is that any way for an executive to act?"

As usual, she'd managed to put him in his place but he did so enjoy messing with her. He'd known how she was going to react before he'd called out to her.

He held up the file folder. "Where is Trip Stanford's background check? It's not in his file."

Crossing her arms, she gave him her patient expression. It was one he knew well.

"Because they're all online now with restricted access. Privacy concerns and all of that. Leann just finished a few weeks ago. Next in line are performance reviews."

"Then there won't be anything in the files," he said, exasperated, tossing the folder back down on the desk. "She might as well digitize everything."

"I think that's the plan, boss. Do you need anything else? A coffee refill?"

His coffee had long ago gone stone cold but he'd been drinking far too much of it lately.

"No, but can you call in my lunch order? The usual."

Grilled chicken on whole wheat with lettuce and tomato. A side of potato salad. Bottle of water. He'd been eating that same lunch for years. If Dizzy knew she'd be horrified.

"You know what? Scratch that order. Make it...I don't know. Surprise me."

Brows pinched together, his assistant was looking at him as if he'd lost his mind.

"Surprise you? Since when do you like surprises? You hate them. You make me tell you in advance when the department is going to sign Happy Birthday to you and bring you cake. You hate Secret Santa at Christmas. You hate doing anything that isn't written on a list first. And now you want me to just order you a random lunch and surprise you? Have you taken up drinking during the day?"

Christ, she made him sound like a major pain in the ass. Which he probably was. He'd found Dizzy just in the nick of time.

Just thinking about her made him happy. He couldn't remember a woman that could do that.

"Stone sober. Seriously, just order something you think I'd like. You know me pretty well after all these years."

Amy's chin lifted and her eyes narrowed suspiciously. "Fine, I will. But I've got my eye on you, Easton. I'm watching and if you're hitting the bottle at breakfast or are a clone sent by the government I'll figure it out."

Why on earth would the government send a clone to take his place? Deciding not to open that can of worms, Easton let Amy go back to her desk while he continued his research into Trip Stanford.

After reading through all of the performance reviews, there was no denying two facts. One was that Trip Stanford was a decent employee. He showed up every day, did his job, and didn't take excessive amounts of sick time. That word mediocre hung in the air, although at times he could do more. If he wanted to.

Which brought Easton to the second fact. When Trip had a female supervisor his performance appraisals were less stellar. Not the kind of behavior that would get him fired but he seemed less likely to volunteer for a project or to work overtime. According to his file, he had at least one tense verbal exchange with each of his female managers while there weren't any when he was working for a man. Interesting.

Trip didn't appear to like it when women reviewed his work or asked him to fix something. This tendency wasn't noted anywhere on the appraisals written by the male supervisor.

Now it could mean that the male manager simply hadn't given a shit if Trip didn't like fixing things so they hadn't documented it but the females did. But he could find out for sure because one of those supervisors still worked at Anderson Industries just down the hall.

If Stanford had trouble dealing with critical females it might explain how that poor woman had ended up dead. Tucking the folder under his arm, Easton headed down the hall to find Trip's former manager. It wouldn't prove anything but it might explain why it happened.

He didn't make it to the other manager's office, however, before his brother Carter exited the elevator and strode down the hall toward him. Carter was supposed to be on a construction site just outside of town.

"What are you—"

"I need to talk to you," Carter interrupted, his expression serious. His lips were pressed together with not a hint of his usual happy go lucky demeanor. "Trip Stanford came up to Dizzy in the grocery store this morning. He hinted that he'd been watching her."

A huge mistake by Stanford, and Easton would put a stop to it immediately. No one was going to hurt Dizzy while he still had breath in his body.

Chapter Twenty-Three

DIZZY HAD THREE angry men in her house, or rather outside of it. Near dinnertime Easton, Carter, and Zach had shown up at her home wearing grim faces and bearing cardboard boxes. She'd eventually found out that those boxes contained motion-activated cameras that they were planning to install around the perimeter of her home. Just in case Trip Stanford was watching her as he'd hinted this morning.

Easton was especially pissed off and he'd been stomping around and growling since he'd arrived. Dizzy's perfectly rational questions about what their plan was had him ranting about how Trip had underestimated the Andersons and overestimated the cops' belief that he was innocent. It had been Zach who had stopped and calmly explained what they were doing. A little while later Leann had joined Dizzy in the living room, drinking wine while the men labored.

"I'm sorry it's come to this," Leann sighed, tucking her legs underneath her where she was perched on the sofa. "But it had to be creepy to talk to Stanford this morning. I saw him at the gas station a few days ago and I couldn't make eye contact. We know what he's done and yet he's walking around just as bold as brass like he's completely innocent. It's maddening that we can't prove it."

Yet. Dizzy hadn't given up and she never would. She'd seen a murder and that wasn't going to fade away like it never happened.

"If he's snooping around these cameras will catch him. Then maybe that will be enough for a warrant to search his house and yard."

"You're the eternal optimist, and I'm the mean pessimist," Leann laughed. "I don't really want Trip to be skulking around but I guess if it puts him on the cops' radar it might be worth it."

"I don't particularly want him on my property either but we've been waiting for him to make a mistake. This might be it."

Easton came back into the house, wiping his hands on an old towel. "We're all done out there. Now we need to get the app set up on your laptop and phone. Mine too. That way we can log in any time day or night and see the footage whether live or archived."

Technology was fascinating and frightening all at the same time. Dizzy loved what the app was capable of but this was the stuff her parents had railed about her entire childhood. Surveillance had been a dirty word in the Foster household and now Dizzy had plunged in with both feet. Thank goodness Tami and Louis were in Greece on an archeological expedition.

With Zach's expertise, it didn't take long to set up the devices that could access the footage. Carter walked around tripping the motion sensors so they could test that every camera worked correctly. The app would also trigger an audible sound on her laptop or phone when any camera was set off. That was going to be a pain in the ass because it didn't have to be a human. A bird, a bunny, or even a stray cat could do it, but it was better to be prepared and a little sleep deprived than not prepared at all and well-rested. If Trip set foot over the property line she, Easton, and Zach were going to know about it within seconds.

"Should I order pizza for everyone?" Dizzy asked when they were finished. She felt much safer with the cameras surrounding her home. "I think I have some coupons around here."

But everyone shook their heads and made their excuses to leave so within a few minutes it was only Dizzy and Easton. Leann and Zach needed some quality couple time and Carter had mumbled something about a date later.

"I can't believe how quickly they all left," Dizzy marveled, giving Easton a questioning look. "It was as if someone had encouraged or flat-out told them to leave. You don't know who that might be, do you?"

"I have no idea," Easton replied with an innocent air. "I think they all just had busy evenings planned. You know how Carter is with his girlfriend of the month. plus Leann and Zach are disgustingly in love."

He wasn't going to confess so she didn't push it. Clearly, the quick exits were planned but she wasn't going to complain about spending more time with Easton all alone.

"I'm sure they did." She dug into the kitchen drawer for takeout menus. "So it's takeout for two, then? What sounds good?"

"Pizza is fine. I'll eat anything so order what you like." He tugged at the neckline of his shirt and wrinkled his nose. "I'm going to take a quick shower before we eat. I worked up a sweat out there despite the temperatures."

Easton clomped up the stairs while she phoned the local pizza parlor, ordering enough food for an army. There could never be too many leftovers in the refrigerator with him around. Placing the phone back down on the counter, she heard the shower running upstairs. Images of Easton stripped down to nothing with water running all over his body had her hurrying toward the stairs.

There was plenty of time. The restaurant was backed up and dinner wouldn't be there for an hour. Plus, a person could never be too clean. A shower sounded like the perfect way to kick off an evening with just the two of them.

✦ ✦ ✦

THE BATHROOM WAS hot and steamy when Dizzy entered it, her blouse immediately clinging to her skin. Easton's naked form was distorted behind the glass shower door but she could see him moving under the spray, rinsing soap from his hair. Apparently, she had her very own sex god rock star because he was singing a Bruce Springsteen song at the top of his lungs. He was pretty damn good too. His cousin Jason sang with a band every now and then but it looked like musical talent ran in the family. But then Easton was probably good at everything he tried.

Quickly stripping off her clothes, she hesitated to swing open the shower door, not wanting to scare him to death. If he slipped and fell she'd never forgive herself, but she couldn't stand here all day either. He didn't take long, drawn-out showers.

"Are you going to come in here with me or stay out there like a creepy stalker?"

So much for surprising him. She stepped into the steam and heat, pressing her body right up against his wet one. "How did you know I was there? I was quiet like a ninja."

Chuckling, he picked up the bottle of body wash. "Baby, you are no ninja. I didn't hear you but I felt you. I think it's part of that spell you put on me. Now I'm already clean but I think we need to get you scrubbed up."

Pouring the liquid into his palm, he then knelt down and rubbed her legs and feet, his rough fingers sending tingles to all the right places. Her knees immediately turned to water and she had to place a hand on the tiled wall to brace herself so she wouldn't fall into a heap on the floor.

"You keep talking about that damn spell. There is no spell. But If I did put a spell on you it would be one where you'd bring me chocolate every day."

Twice a day when she was PMSing. Maybe some wine too. And ice cream. But the part about feeling that she was close by was kind of sweet and romantic.

He didn't reply, intent on his task of washing every inch of her flesh. His hands glided down her back and over her bottom. He seemed to take a long time washing her breasts, especially the pebble-like nipples that he worried with his thumbs until she was moving restlessly on her feet.

"You're doing a very...thorough...job," she gasped, sucking air into her aching lungs with every syllable. "I didn't even...need...a shower."

"But you needed this," Easton purred into her ear, lifting her up and pressing her back again the wall. "Don't you, baby?"

Wrapping her legs around his hips, she braced her hands on

his wide shoulders as he entered her in one hard thrust, filling her completely. "Stop talking and give it to me. Hard."

And he did. Repeatedly. Again and again, each stroke rubbing her sweet spot until she thought she would scream with the pleasure. Squeezing her eyes shut, there was nothing in the world at the moment except Easton pounding into her, the spray of the water running down her overheated flesh and his lips plundering her own. It was sensation overload and she couldn't take much more. Liquid heat ran through her veins and she tossed her head back and forth as the pressure built in her abdomen. She couldn't take much more but her orgasm was just outside of her reach, mere millimeters from her fingertips.

Frustration made her groan and cry out his name but then he was there – exactly where she needed him to be – circling her clit until her toes curled and her climax exploded. Her body shook with its force and she barely registered his own release, so lost in the waves of bliss from her own.

Much later when they were back on earth, he slowly lowered her feet to the floor, holding her steady on legs that felt like jelly. Eventually she was able to balance on her own and she allowed him to finish washing her, this time efficiently rather than sensuously. Docilely, she followed him out of the shower and stood quietly while he dried them both off. He pulled on a pair of sweatpants and a t-shirt but wrapped her in her warm robe before lifting her into his arms and carrying her to the bed.

Snuggling close, she breathed in his clean scent that was already mixing with the shower gel. It was warm, manly, and clean and she couldn't get enough of it, pressing her nose to the cords of his neck and inhaling until her lungs were full of him.

"What are you doing, baby?"

"Smelling you."

His chest rumbled with laughter at her silly answer. "Smelling me? Why?"

"Because you smell good," she replied simply, a yawn escaping that she couldn't hold back. It had been a long day. "Take it as a compliment."

"I do. I'm just not sure how to feel about it, but I do admit that I like the way you smell too."

"It's primitive. It's the animal in us that's attracted to scent."

His brows pinched together in a frown. "You mean if I didn't smell this way you might have ended up with someone else?"

"Doubtful. I like the way you look too." Her limbs were heavy but she managed to sit up on the bed. Literally the last thing she wanted to do was get up but the pizza delivery would be showing up at the front door any minute. "I need to get dressed. Dinner will be here very soon."

"Can we have our pizza in bed?"

They could. She'd had pizza in bed while watching television too many times to count.

"I've created a monster," she teased. "You've gone from an uptight workaholic to a man who never wants to get out of bed. Anderson Industries will never be the same."

He sat up and surveyed the room, his gaze running from left to right and then back again.

"I'll run the entire empire from here. Video conferences and email can handle it. Then I can keep you naked in bed right beside me."

Uh…no. He hadn't thought this through.

"If I'm naked, maybe those conferences shouldn't be video."

"There are a few flaws in my plan but I think I'm on to something here." He grinned and then dropped a kiss on her lips. "I have another plan for after we eat our pizza."

She'd bet anything that his plan looked a hell of a lot like hers. Neither one of them were going to get much sleep tonight. But it would be worth it.

Chapter Twenty-Four

IZZY AWOKE TO the most annoying beeping sound she'd ever heard and all she wanted to do was make it stop so she could go back to sleep. She and Easton had been up half the night exploring each other's bodies and he'd found and catalogued every spot of flesh that when caressed sent her eyes rolling back into her head. But he'd promised that if he'd missed a spot or two they could do it all over again the next night. It was a promise without making a big production about it. It was Easton's way of saying that he was here and wasn't going anywhere. Her heart had melted when he'd said it.

But that damn beeping was still ringing in her ears and she lifted her eyelids, heavy from fatigue only to see that Easton had already levered up from the bed and had his phone in his hand. Distracted by the very fine view of his naked backside, it took her a minute to realize that it was the new app that was making that noise. Someone was on her property. Maybe Trip?

Hopping out of bed, she grabbed her robe and dragged it on, not bothering to smooth her hair or put on shoes. If Trip was in her yard, she certainly wasn't going to dress up just for him. Easton had managed to pull on a pair of boxers and in his hand was the gun he'd placed on the nightstand last night before they'd fallen asleep. She wasn't a huge fan of firearms but she had to concede that in this case she felt much better knowing he was armed.

"Just stay here," Easton commanded as he paged through the camera angles on the phone looking for the right one. "It's probably just a rabbit or a bird, but I need to make sure."

Oh hell no.

"I'm not staying behind," she hissed, tying the sash on her robe. "If Trip is out there I'm not going to cower in my bed."

He scowled at his phone. "I'm not seeing anything. Just stay here. There's no reason for both of us to freeze our asses off. I'll be right back."

The sound of Dizzy's front door opening and then voices carried up the stairs and Easton immediately pushed her behind him. "Stay here."

She did as she was told but something wasn't quite right. In the dead of night it had been so quiet she'd heard the click of the deadbolt. Whoever was in her house…well…it sounded like he had a key. And those voices? There were two distinct people and they sounded familiar.

Leann and Zach? No, it wouldn't be them. Then…shit. Double shit.

She tried to grab at Easton's arm to stay his movements but before she could stop him he was heading downstairs with a gun in his hand. This was bad. So very bad. They hadn't yet invented a word for how terrible this was about to be. Poor Easton had no clue what he was walking into and she couldn't stop him.

Hurrying behind him, they both paused at the bottom of the

stairs as a lamp came to life with a click, illuminating the living room and the people that had turned on the light. Easton's mouth hung open and Dizzy could only place her hand on the arm that held the gun, pushing it down.

Because it was in poor taste to point a firearm at her peace-loving, pacifist parents. Tami and Louis Foster had arrived unexpectedly and they were standing in the middle of her living room surrounded by luggage and staring at herself and Easton. They appeared too shocked to say anything after finding their daughter spending the night with a half-naked man. She was sure she looked the part of a wanton too, with her hair standing on end and her lips swollen from the night's activities, plus Easton wearing nothing but boxers. This was so screwed up and the silence stretched on. It was up to Dizzy to break the tension. Except that she sucked at stuff like that.

"Tami. Louis. Nice to see you. You remember Easton Anderson?"

✦   ✦   ✦

EASTON WAS IN the living room making awkward small talk with Dizzy's father while she made coffee with her mother in the kitchen. After greeting her parents, she'd found out that they'd flown back to the States as soon as they could wrap up their work when they'd heard about the murder next door from her latest email. They were here to… What she didn't really know. Protect her? She'd told them in the email that she had that covered. Help her prove Trip killed someone? The closest Tami and Louis had ever come to a murder investigation were the Agatha Christie novels they liked to read. Maybe they were simply tired of Greece and looking for a reason to leave?

Tami slapped the coffee filter into the basket, not looking at her only child. "It's not that I care that you were in bed with a man, Dizzy. That's not it at all. We're sexual beings and of course you have needs like any other woman. We raised you not to be ashamed of your sexuality but to embrace it. Celebrate it."

They sure had and boy, had it been embarrassing as hell when she'd dated in high school. She'd wanted to hide when a boy would pick her up and they'd tell him that Dizzy didn't have curfews because she had to learn to make good decisions by making a bunch of bad ones. That teenager had quickly realized he was considered a *bad* one. And then there had been that time her mother had asked her when she turned fifteen if she wanted to go on the pill. It wouldn't have been so bad but they were all at the diner and Leann had been sitting there too.

Tami shook her head and finally her gaze landed on Dizzy, her expression stormy. "I can understand casual sex. Lord knows, I had my share before I met your father. I can understand exploring different lifestyles. But I cannot understand this. I thought we raised you better than this."

Tami was acting like Dizzy was the killer, not Trip.

"You've put about four scoops too many in the coffeemaker. You'll be able to clean the toilets with that."

Dizzy's idea of a joke fell flat. Tami didn't crack a smile.

"I hope it poisons me," she said dramatically. "I can't believe what I saw tonight. My daughter having sex with a...with a...millionaire capitalist."

Her mother shuddered with distaste and scooped some of the coffee out of the filter and back into the container.

"That man stands for everything we loathe. He's all about making more money and building the family empire. We were okay with you being friends with the Andersons but did you have to sleep with one too?" Tami threw up her hands. "Where did we go wrong as parents?"

It made sense now. Of course, Tami and Louis didn't care that they'd practically caught their little girl fornicating outside of marriage. That wasn't an issue. It was that Easton was one of *those* Andersons. The one percenters. Part of the corporate oligarchy. The upper class.

"Would you rather I shag a penniless artist? Would that make you feel better, Tami?"

Her mother slammed down a coffee cup she was retrieving from the cabinet. "At least he wouldn't be part of the systematic disintegration of workers' rights in this country."

Dizzy hadn't had much sleep and she was out of practice dealing with her parents but she still remembered when it was time to put her foot down. If she didn't, Tami could go on and on all night about this and frankly, Dizzy didn't have the patience. Or the energy.

"You know that the Andersons are good and decent people and that they treat their employees very well. I can assure you that Easton isn't trying to chip away at their rights, nor is he lining his pockets by making shoddy products or fighting against fair compensation."

Pressing her hands together, Tami's eyes were bright with unshed tears. "Did it have to be a rich man? You couldn't find a poor man to love? Did you even try? And don't tell me you don't love him. He wouldn't have been here all night if you didn't. Oh my God, are you two engaged? Are you going to marry him?"

For just a brief second, Dizzy wanted to say yes, she was marrying Easton and they were going to live in a big mansion with servants and have lots of little capitalist children that would go into the family business or just live off of their trust funds, adding nothing to the betterment of society.

But she didn't.

Dizzy pressed the power button on the coffeemaker. "I am not marrying him. We haven't been dating long. But if I were, you need to know that Easton is a good man and is not defined by his bank balance."

"But you're in love with him," Tami persisted. "You are, aren't you?"

In love. Two simple words. Six letters. Not a big deal but somehow they really packed a wallop when said out loud.

Did she love Easton?

And if she did, did he love her back?

This was why she avoided dating most of the time. The uncertainty was terrible.

"I am not going to discuss that with you when you're in this mood," Dizzy said instead of answering the question. "If I say no, you won't believe me and if I say yes, you'll have a stroke. I can't win either way."

"This is his doing. You would have answered me before dating him. He's changed you already."

Yes, Dizzy had changed from a little girl to a grown woman but her mother and father had been too busy gallivanting around the globe to notice. They believed in freedom of expression but at this moment they weren't acting like that.

"I've changed." Dizzy pointed to herself. "Me, Tami. Just me. This doesn't have anything to do with Easton and everything to do with *me*. You brought me up to be whatever I wanted to be and do what I please, not caring what other people thought. Well...you're other people too. This is who I have become and it isn't because of Easton. I was this person before but you were too busy digging up relics and protesting corporate mergers to notice. I'm a part of you and Louis, but I'm my own person as well. If you can't respect the decisions I've made in my life then I'm sorry, but I'm not going to change. Not for you or anybody."

Dizzy had rarely stood up to her parents – had rarely needed to as they were permissive to a fault – but she wouldn't let this go without saying something. The Andersons were her second family and wonderful people.

"I don't want to be another version of you," Dizzy said gently to her mother. "Honestly, I'm not sure the world could handle two of you."

Tami played with the handle of the cup and then gave her daughter a half-smile. "I guess that would be frightening for most people. I can be quite formidable when I want to be."

"You can," Dizzy agreed. "Now can we go out there and be nice to Easton? He's a good man, Tami. Kind and wonderful. Smart and funny. I really like him."

Rubbing her forehead, Tami sighed loudly. "You mean you love him." Dizzy opened her mouth to object but Tami held up her hand. "Fine, you just like him a lot. Okay, I'll be nice but if he brings up politics or the state of the wealth gap in the United States or the importance of worker representation, I'm going to let him have it with both barrels."

If Easton had any brains at all he wouldn't touch those subjects, or any like them with a ten-foot pole.

"I wouldn't expect anything less."

He could hold his own, Dizzy was sure of that. He'd be fine. But there was one question that was still niggling in the back of her mind…

Did she love Easton Anderson?

Chapter Twenty-Five

A FTER TRAVELING ALL night and through several time zones, Dizzy's parents were happy to lie down in the guest room, giving her some much-needed space to talk to Easton. He was fixing breakfast and doing his best not to look or talk to her, an action she didn't understand. Why was he upset? It was her parents that had shown up unannounced. She was the one that should be banging pots and pans around. She loved her parents dearly but they could make her crazy without even trying. The good residents of Tremont thought she was strange? They'd forgotten about Tami and Louis. They made her look downright normal.

"What did those eggs ever do to you?"

Easton's back was to her but she could easily see his knuckles turn white as he tightly gripped the spatula's handle. Good thing she liked scrambled eggs because with his mood that was all she was going to get. No over easy. No sunny side up.

He lifted the frying pan off of the burner and scooped the eggs onto two plates, joining the toast Dizzy had pulled from the toaster. They'd settled at the kitchen table and Easton dug into his breakfast as if he hated those eggs, stabbing them with his fork over and over. Deciding she wouldn't push, she began to eat her own meal but her gaze kept flickering back to him to gauge his expression. Food was not helping his mood. Eventually, he'd cleaned his plate and he didn't have much choice but to speak.

"Your parents hate my guts. No, scratch that. They hate my entire family."

Finally. With relief, she set her own fork down on the edge of the plate and wiped her mouth with a napkin.

"To be fair, they don't hate you personally. They hate your money."

"They'd like it better if I was broke?"

"Yes."

He was looking at her as if she'd lost her mind. "Because that would make me a better, more honest person? That's bullshit. I'd still be me. Money doesn't make me a bad person."

"Of course, it doesn't," Dizzy assured him. "This is just Tami and Louis's political views run amuck. Just be patient with them. It's easy to hate a faceless international conglomerate but once they get to know you, they'll like you. I'm sure of it. They like Leann."

"They probably think she's adopted." He sprang from the chair and went to the coffee pot to refill their cups. "I don't like having to apologize to your folks for who and what I am. The Anderson family does a lot of good for this town. Do they know that?"

"They do. They're just fired up these days, far more than usual. Like I said, just let them get to know you. Everything will be fine. I told them what a great person you are."

"I heard and I do appreciate that," he replied curtly, although it didn't sound like he appreciated it. "In fact, I heard the whole conversation. It turns out your dad isn't so chatty. He said something to me about using birth control and then that was pretty much it. I tried to engage him but we ended up discussing the weather and school starting up soon."

"Louis isn't much of a talker," she sighed. "Tami handles that most of the time. It works well for them."

"In the thirty-plus years that they've been married I doubt the poor man has been able to get in a word edgewise."

Dizzy pushed her plate away. She didn't like his tone. They were her parents, after all.

"Now wait a minute. That is my mother you're talking about. Whatever they're doing in their marriage it's obviously working, so I don't think we should be second-guessing what goes on between a husband and wife."

Easton put his plate in the sink with a clatter. "If he starts complaining, she probably just tells him he's happy. Is he allowed to have his own thoughts?"

Standing, she cleared her own breakfast dishes and then brushed by Easton to place them in the dishwasher. He needed to simmer down and quick. She understood that he was upset but badmouthing her parents wasn't the way to deal with it.

They were her parents. For good or bad. They were a handful but their heart was in the right place. They truly just wanted world peace and to end hunger.

"Once he gets to know you my dad will talk your ear off about anything and everything, but he just met you. Give him and my mother a break. You're not exactly a talkative extrovert. Most of the time you don't even want to be around people."

"Because I have work to do." He sounded exasperated but Dizzy didn't give a shit. He was being a jerk. "It's completely different."

Exhaling slowly, she thought carefully about her next words. This entire conversation had gone off the rails so quickly. "Listen, I know more than anyone that my parents can be difficult. They won't be here forever, though. They'll quickly get bored and they'll leave for another dig or a demonstration or something like it. While they're here I won't let them interfere in my life, I can assure you of that. They raised me to be independent and that's exactly what I am. They can have an opinion as can everyone else but I don't have to live my life according to their whims. Honestly, Easton, they're hardly here. Just ignore them."

Apparently, she'd chosen the wrong words because Easton threw up his hands in frustration. "Sure, this time they'll leave, but they'll be back. At holidays. Birthday celebrations. *They hate me.* Full stop. And they hate my family. My family, Dizzy. And you don't seem to care at all."

Of course, she cared but he had blown their influence out of proportion. They were only two people.

"Because I've lived with them for thirty years," she explained, keeping her tone as calm as possible when all she really wanted to do was slap him on the back of the head. "I understand them and they don't hate anyone, Easton. They truly don't. They may not *approve* of you but they don't hate you or your family. Can't you trust me on this? It will all be okay."

It was clear that he couldn't. A muscle jumped in his jaw and he was pacing around her small kitchen like it was a prison cell.

Finally, he turned back to her, his expression sad.

"I just can't help but believe that this is going to be a problem going forward. How can we build any sort of relationship and future knowing that your parents don't approve of me and my family? And who are they to judge me, anyway? What gives them that right?"

"Nothing in the world," she assured him. "They're no worse or better than anyone else on this planet. They have strong ideas about things but they'll come around. I'm just asking for your patience. When they come back downstairs I'll have them apologize to you, then I'll plan a nice dinner with them and your family. Everybody will get along fine. They were just surprised today."

No one seemed to care that she'd been surprised too. Coming to grips with Tami and Louis sleeping in her guest room was something that she usually had a few weeks or even months to get used to.

"I don't want a forced apology," Easton said stiffly, his gaze dropping to the tile floor. "I think that maybe we should back off a little while your parents are here."

It was as if his words had sucked all the oxygen out of the room and she was left struggling for breath. It took effort to speak but she managed to find her voice.

"You mean you want to take a break?"

Shoving his hands in his pockets, Easton still didn't make eye contact. Asshole.

"Just while your parents are here."

The back of her neck was hot and anger had her stomach churning. "And then?"

"We can start seeing each other again."

He had to know he was being a giant pussy because he couldn't look her in the eye.

"I have a better idea. Why don't you go fuck yourself?"

His head snapped up and finally she could see his expression. A little fear, a little annoyance, and a whole lot of uncertainty.

And if he'd decided to express any of that to her, she would have cut him some slack, but since he was acting like a total asshole all bets were off.

"Excuse me?"

"I'll be happy to explain." She sounded sarcastic as hell but she was too pissed off to tell. "If I'm not worth hanging in there for, then I don't think you care about me enough. If you don't want to work this out, then you probably won't want to work anything out. Every time we have a problem you'll disappear until it's moot. That's not a partner, that's a magician disappearing into the ether when life gets a little tough. As lovely as your idea sounds, I'll think I'll pass. I don't like conditional relationships."

There was an answering spark of anger in his blue eyes and his face was red. Good, she'd made him mad.

"Listen, it's *your* parents–"

"Who are a lovely and convenient excuse for you," she cut in, tears burning the back of her eyes. Her heart hurt in her chest and there wasn't anything she could do to stop it. She'd allowed herself to be vulnerable and this was the result. "Why do I have the feeling this isn't about Tami and Louis? I think this is about you, Easton. This isn't about my parents not liking you. This is all about you and how uncomfortable you would feel escorting me to one of your godawful boring business cocktail parties. This is about me being on your arm when you meet the governor at a charity function. This is about me believing in psychics and ESP and the rhythm of the universe. This is about my being an artist and not a businesswoman. And this is damn sure about you having cold feet about being serious with someone who has crazy ass ideas. This is you using them as an excuse to pull back when things are getting too damn real."

His reply was low, almost a whisper. "It's not an excuse."

All the anger had drained out of her. She had nothing left. If Easton didn't want to fight for her and their relationship, there wasn't much left to say. A few tears slipped down her cheeks and she dashed at them with the back of her hand.

"Here's the thing…you might be using them as an excuse or you might not. But the results are the same. You're leaving, pulling away and putting us on hold until a more convenient time. If that ever comes. I guess I'm supposed to just wait here until you come back, but that's the one thing I can't do. I'm all in, Easton. I'm here and ready to make it work. But you have to be all in too. I'm worth more than halfway."

Her heart pounded in her ears as she waited for him to speak. It looked like for a moment he was going to and then he turned away toward the stairs. It was then that she remembered that Easton cared what other people thought of him. He cared that her parents didn't seem to like him. It also reminded him that there might be others who shared their feelings, and he didn't like that at all. And that reminded him of how his friends and business acquaintances would look at her. She was *eccentric*, after all, and she didn't have a stock portfolio.

"I need to go to the office. I'll talk to you later about security for tonight."

The office. That magical place where Easton was completely in control and knew exactly what to do and say.

"My parents are here. I'll be fine."

She would be fine. It was her heart that was in pieces, and that wouldn't mend anytime soon.

Chapter Twenty-Six

E ASTON HAD ARRIVED at the office at the same time Zach was dropping Leann off. He'd invited both of them up to his office, knowing he needed to discuss the situation with Dizzy. There were plans that needed to be made. His assistant fetched them three coffees and he explained what had happened and managed not to go into too much detail or blame Dizzy for overreacting.

For the first time that Easton could remember, the office didn't feel like the haven it had always been. Even now he was unsettled, still thinking about his argument with Dizzy. Normally he would have shaken it off and be deep into his work by now.

But then this wasn't any ordinary situation and Dizzy wasn't an ordinary woman.

"You did what?" Leann shrieked when he was done, her eyes wide and her cheeks bright red. "Have you lost your mind?"

Easton had been wondering that exact thing since he'd left Dizzy's house less than an hour ago. That conversation hadn't gone at all the way he'd planned. He'd assumed that he and Dizzy wouldn't see each other while her parents were in town but she'd taken it as a rejection of their entire relationship and even accused him of not caring enough for her. She thought he was using her mom and dad as an excuse because they were moving too fast.

He was pretty sure that he wasn't doing that. Almost. But they were moving quickly by his usual standards, although this was different. He'd known Dizzy for years.

"I have not lost my mind but thank you for asking." He turned his attention to Zach, who had stayed quiet while he'd explained what had happened. He and Dizzy might have broken up this morning but he still wanted to make sure she was safe. "Now I just want to make sure that someone is watching Dizzy. She says she'll be okay because her parents are there but I'm not so sure. If I can't be there, someone should."

"I'll watch over her."

Easton looked up to see Carter strolling into his office. Where in the hell was his assistant? She was supposed to be monitoring his visitors, although to be fair he rarely refused to see any of his brothers.

"Why would you do that?"

Carter stood between Leann and Zach, who were sitting on the opposite side of Easton's desk. His jaw was jutted forward in an aggressive stance and his arms were crossed over his chest. All in all, he didn't look happy. Too fucking bad. Easton had more pressing problems than his little brother's emotional wellbeing.

"Because someone needs to, obviously. Looks like you got tired of playing house."

Standing, Easton came around the desk so he could look his brother in the eye. He didn't like it when anyone hovered over him. "It's a very complicated situation and I don't have time to explain it to you."

"I heard enough," Carter said shortly. "Dizzy's parents don't think much of us Andersons and you got all butthurt. Is that about it?"

Easton needed this bullshit like he needed a hole in the head. "All I did—"

"All you did was make Dizzy believe you didn't care enough," Leann said, jumping from her chair. "That you didn't love her enough to deal with her family, which is bullshit, by the way, because she's never complained about dealing with ours."

"Why would she complain?" It didn't make any sense. "Our family is wonderful."

Zach was smiling now, chuckling behind his hand. Leann nudged him with her foot.

"Tell him, handsome."

"The Andersons are wonderful." Zach seemed sincere but there was a mischievous gleam in his eye. "And nosy, and bossy, and judgmental when it comes down to dating the only female. Don't get me wrong, I love your family. But nobody circles the wagons quicker than the Andersons, and heaven help you if one of them is mad at you because then they're all mad at you. When Leann and I have a disagreement I have every Anderson male in my office telling me what I need to do, how I need to do it, and when I need to do it. Then they come back later to check on me and make sure I did it."

Smiling, Leann leaned down to kiss her boyfriend. "But I'm worth it."

"Yes, honey, you are. No question there."

Scraping his fingers through his hair, Easton sighed. "I just suggested a break. That's it. She's the one that blew it all out of proportion. She accused me of not caring and then she said that I was using her parents as an excuse to back out of the relationship because we were moving too fast. She said that I'm uncomfortable dating a woman that believes in psychics."

"And are you?" Carter asked, his brows raised. "Is she right? Because I'd be proud to have a woman like Dizzy in my life. If you two are on a break, I think I'll give her a call and ask her out."

It had been one long and miserable fucking morning and Easton had pretty much lost the little patience that he'd had when he woke up. Still it was a surprise when he realized it was his fist connecting with his little brother's jaw. Pain shot up his arm as Carter's body flew backward along with a few file folders from Easton's desk, the papers fluttering as they fell to the floor. He shouldn't have done it but dammit, Carter was getting on his last nerve.

It wasn't as if this was the first time he'd punched Carter. Probably wouldn't be the last, either. The brothers were known to take out their frustrations on each other.

Sprawled on the carpet, Carter rubbed his face and laughed, not appearing to be too upset that he'd been punched in the face. Leann and Zach had moved to the other side of the room, not wanting to be in the middle of two fighting Anderson boys.

"You love her. Just admit it, say you're sorry, and then she'll forgive you," Carter said, levering to his feet. "What are you waiting for?"

"It doesn't matter." Easton's shoulders slumped. No one seemed to be understanding the issue. "Her parents still hate me, and they hate you too, by the way, so don't bother to ask her out. They hate everything we stand for."

The office was quiet until Zach cleared his throat. "Sounds like this is a family matter, so I think I'll run over to Dizzy's and check on her. See how she's doing. It will give me a chance to check out Stanford's house as well. See if he's dug any new flowerbeds lately." He leaned down and dropped a quick kiss on Leann's cheek. "I'll call you later, baby."

After Zach left, Leann turned and gave Easton and Carter a nasty look. "Both of you better straighten up because I have lost patience. This is a matter of life and death for Dizzy and you're letting your testosterone do the thinking for you. Carter, I love you but stay away from Dizzy. No one needs you muddying up the waters right now." She shook her finger under Easton's nose. "And as for you, I don't give a shit if her parents hire a hit man to take you out, you're going to nut up and deal with it. She needs us right now and you do not have the luxury of acting like a diva. Are you listening to me? Because I'm serious here. You're going to fix this with her, and that means admitting to yourself why you did it."

Easton held up his hands in surrender. "I'm listening. Jesus, you're bossy. I feel sorry for Zach. And I told you why I did it."

"And not one person believes you," Leann replied smoothly with a bright smile. "I doubt you do either. Now stop being a jerk and be the man I know you can be. I need to get back to my own office. I have a meeting in ten minutes. Some of us don't have the luxury of playing *Fight Club* on a workday."

Turning on her heel, Leann was gone in a second leaving Carter and Easton alone. It looked like his brother's jaw was going to bruise. Their parents would find out about this. Shit. Easton was a grown man but he could still be cowed by his mother's disappointed expression and his father's disapproval.

"I can have my assistant get you some ice."

Chuckling, Carter rubbed at it. "If that's your half-assed way of saying you're sorry, then I accept your lame apology."

"I am sorry." Easton knew better than to turn on a brother but that's how they were. He'd hit the one guy he knew would take it. "This entire situation has me twisted up. I don't want to hurt Dizzy but I don't want to be hurt either. What if her parents convince her that I'm not good for her?"

Strolling toward the door, Carter just gave him a grin. "What if they don't?"

Easton fell back into his leather chair when his brother left, images of this morning with Dizzy crowding out any other thoughts, leaving him with little urge to work and less ability to do so. He wanted to believe in what they had together but her parents had brought up some valid points.

They *were* different. Very different. Dizzy had a far different view of the world than he did. Could they make it? Could they find some middle ground to build a relationship on? Would she grow tired of him eventually? She was the creative and interesting one, after all. He was...disgustingly normal. There wasn't anything much special about him.

Did it matter either way? Because he'd only been without Dizzy for a few hours and already he was missing her. Somehow he had to find a way to make this work.

Chapter Twenty-Seven

"C AN I GET you some coffee, Zach?"

Zach had stopped by the house this morning and Dizzy wondered just how much he knew about her argument with Easton. He didn't act or say anything outwardly but it was the way he was skirting the subject that made her suspicious. Also, he was here discussing how they planned to keep her safe. If he thought that Easton was still spending nights here, he wouldn't have bothered.

"Thank you, that's very kind." Zach's gaze lingered on the stairway. "Are your parents here?"

Yep, he knew. That meant Leann knew too. Dizzy needed to fire up her phone. She probably had a dozen or so messages from her best friend.

"They were but they're out taking a walk trying to fend off the desire to sleep. Jet lag," she explained. "They took a short nap but they're still exhausted so they thought a walk might help. They'll probably be gone for awhile, especially if they see anyone they know. They'll want to catch up on all the town gossip."

Dizzy carried the steaming cup of java out to her visitor.

"Here you go—"

At some point this morning, Dizzy had turned on the television as background noise. Now her attention was captured by a commercial and she set the mug down on the coffee table and then moved closer to the television to watch it more closely. A woman in a blue blazer and skirt stood in front of a newer home probably from one of the Anderson's developments. Blonde and smiling, she appeared to be in her early to mid-thirties and advertising a local real estate business just one town over. There were two other people in the closing shot, a man and a woman in blazers matching the first woman's. They were realtors who wanted Dizzy to list her house with them or allow them to find her dream home.

"Dizzy," Zach said softly, finally dragging her gaze back to him now that the commercial was over. "Are you okay? You're white as a sheet. Are you ill?"

Still dazed and unsure of what she'd seen, she sat down on the floor, her legs too shaky to hold her up. Sweat had popped out on her forehead and her breath was coming in ragged gasps.

I couldn't have just seen that.

But I did.

"I'm not sick." She looked up at Zach, who was of course puzzled by her behavior. She could see his concern growing when she didn't elaborate.

"Okay…you seem upset, though. Do you want to talk about it?"

Dizzy most certainly did want to discuss it but she wasn't sure how to begin. It was like seeing a ghost.

"The woman in the commercial. The pretty blonde one. She

was the woman I saw in Trip's house that night. She was the one murdered."

✦ ✦ ✦

ZACH HAD CALLED his boss Jason after Dizzy's revelation about the identity of the woman in the window. He'd hurried over along with Leann and Easton so now there was a great deal of talking – mostly over each other – and not much listening. Easton and Jason were speaking loudly, going back and forth, debating what to do next while Zach was outside, checking on the perimeter of the house and trying to get a good look at Trip's home.

Dizzy and Leann took refuge in the kitchen making more hot chocolates. Double marshmallows. This was probably going to get worse before it got better. Tami and Louis would be home soon and they'd add to the mayhem. It was bad enough that Easton had shown up. The tension in the room was sky high. They'd barely looked at each other.

Leann sighed and stirred her cocoa as they rejoined the men in the living room. "They might go on like this all day. Maybe we should order pizza. I'm getting hungry."

The mention of food had the two men quiet for the first time in almost half an hour.

"I don't need pizza," Jason replied. "Brinley's cooking dinner. I just need Easton to listen to me."

"I am listening," the other man growled. "But you aren't making any sense. We have to call the police."

"And tell them what? That you've identified the victim of the murder that they don't even believe happened?"

"If the woman is missing that lends credence to my claim," Dizzy pointed out. "They'd have to do something then."

The back door opened and Zach entered, wiping his feet on the mat and holding up his phone. "I think Jared found some information that might help our case with the police. Turns out Trip has a record with the university cops where he went to school. Assault and battery and stalking. Our Trip has a dark side."

Dizzy had never been so relieved to find out that someone was dangerous but it confirmed everything that she'd been feeling and seeing. "He beat someone up?"

Zach nodded. "He has multiple complaints from females. They didn't show up in a regular background check because the two systems weren't linked. But Jared found something else that might interest the cops. I sent him the picture of our victim once Dizzy identified her and he did a reverse search. It didn't take long to find her. She's a member of the same online dating service that Stanford is. Some coincidence. Her name is Janine Erskine. She's twenty-nine and lives in Rowland, about twenty miles from here. Never married and no kids, although according to her profile she's thinking about getting a cat. She likes camping, hiking, and watching old movies."

"That could be how they met," Dizzy said, but she wasn't happy or excited. Now that the face had a name and a personality she could only be sad. Janine had been a real person with goals and dreams. Trip had taken that away from her.

"Good work," Jason said. "That should be enough to convince the cops to talk to Trip."

"And if they don't," Easton growled, his brows pinched together. "We'll get West to tell them to. Technically he's their boss."

"I don't think we want to get in the habit of having West intervene," cautioned Jason. "If we can't get the police to listen to us then we need to up our game and get the evidence they need. Personally, I think we have enough for them to question Trip, maybe even get a search warrant, although I don't want us to get ahead of ourselves. This is far from over. I doubt Trip is going to fall apart and confess if the cops bring him in. That doesn't happen near as much in reality as it does on television."

Jason pulled out his phone and dialed the chief of police, leaving Dizzy with Zach, Leann, and Easton. Just two cozy couples. No, make that one couple and two people who weren't speaking to one another.

She *had* told him to go fuck himself. That might have been a bit of an over-reaction but she wasn't backing down from what she'd said. This was Easton caring too much about what other people thought. They were happy together but he had to go and find the fly in the ointment. She could have talked to her parents and told them to back off but he'd blown it all out of proportion. She still felt it was much more than just her mom and dad. Easton was afraid of what it would be like if she was truly his girlfriend. Apparently, he thought she was going to strip down and dance naked under a full moon while at some snotty dinner party.

Idiot. Everyone knew that silver robes were the garment of choice for a ceremony under the full moon. It was a new moon that liked nudity.

"So..." Easton rocked on his heels, his hands stuffed deeply into his pockets. "I guess I should be going. Are you and Zach staying here tonight, Leann?"

The prick still hadn't looked at her. If he wanted to be that way, then fine. She could ignore the hell out of him too.

Her gaze darting back and forth between Dizzy and Easton, Leann cleared her throat.

"We are. We're taking Dizzy's room and she's going to sleep on the couch, although we keep telling her that we could sleep down here on an air mattress. She won't listen."

The third bedroom didn't have a bed and was used for storage, but considering all the people that seemed to want to spend the night in her house she might have to get a bed for that room.

"That's right. I won't. You're guests here."

Plus Tami and Louis. They were a whole other issue.

"If that's settled, I think I'll go." Easton practically ran to the door, anxious to escape. He muttered some goodbyes and then he was gone, gunning the engine of his SUV as he drove away.

"I'm sorry you had to witness that," Dizzy said, closing the front door. She'd let the cold air into the house again. "As you know we had a disagreement this morning. I said some things. He said some things. Now we can't take them back. Maybe we don't want to, either. Suffice it to say, it's awkward as hell between us."

Leann picked put the two mugs of hot chocolate. "I hope you told Easton he's a dumbass."

Dizzy felt the heat rise in her cheeks. "I told him to go fuck himself. Not my finest moment."

Zach winced and shuddered. "Ouch. I can't imagine that he took it well. He was still upset when we talked to him in his office."

"He deserved it," Leann said smugly. "Long past due, if you ask me."

Dizzy threw up her hands in frustration. "But now what? He wouldn't even look at me, let alone talk this through."

"He will." Leann seemed confident in that statement. "Just give him time. He'll realize he's being stupid and come running to apologize."

Her parents were going to do the same, they just didn't know it yet. Since retiring five years ago, they'd become far more judgmental than they'd ever been. It was getting out of hand and they were going to lose friends if they weren't careful.

Eventually she was going to have to have it out with them.

Chapter Twenty-Eight

SMOOTHING DOWN HER black pencil skirt, Dizzy checked her white blouse for coffee stains after she placed her cup in the dishwasher. She was going to the Anderson building and she was sure to see Easton today, so she wanted to look as put together as possible. She didn't want him to think she'd tossed and turned all night, barely sleeping because they'd fought.

That's why she'd used a ton of makeup. To cover the dark circles. She might know how terrible her night was but he didn't have to.

"You're all dressed up," Tami remarked, joining her in the kitchen. Dizzy's mother was dressed in casual sweatpants and a Grateful Dead t-shirt, her hair pulled up on top of her head. She looked much younger than her chronological age, but then she'd always acted and looked young. "Where are you going?"

Irritation rose up but Dizzy slapped it down quickly. Her mother didn't mean anything by the question. She wasn't the type to ever check up on her daughter, even though it kind of came out that way. Tami wasn't the mothering type, worried about her child. Dizzy could have stayed out all night when she was fifteen and her parents would have simply put it down to *expressing herself.*

This also wasn't the moment to start a conversation about judging people and Easton in particular. She didn't have time to hash it out with them. That was another thing that had kept Dizzy from sleeping. She needed to deal with Tami and Louis. If they were going to stay here for any length of time, they needed to be cordial to her friends.

"I'm heading over to Anderson Industries with Zach." Dizzy nodded toward the stairs. "He's getting ready now. We're all gathering there to wait for a call from the police after they question Trip."

Leann had already left earlier for a meeting so Zach had stayed with Dizzy, not wanting her to be left alone now that Trip had been contacted by the police. They'd called him last night and invited him in today for what they were calling a *discussion*. Zach was afraid that it might set off Trip so now Dizzy had to have a babysitter all the time instead of just at night.

Tami walked over to the back windows and lifted the curtain to look out. "Does he think Trip is dangerous?"

More irritation. This was becoming a habit. But the longer her mom and dad stayed away the more used to living without them Dizzy became. "Of course he thinks Trip is dangerous. He killed a woman, Tami. He's a murderer and I'm the lone witness. Isn't that why you came home?"

Her reply had come out harsher than she'd planned but her nerves were on a razor's edge lately.

Tami turned and frowned, her gaze running up and down her daughter. "Yes, that's why we came back but clearly you need to relax. When you return, we'll light some candles and meditate. It will clear your mind and spirit. You could try a juice fast as well. Flush the toxins out of your system along with all of that negative energy you're holding onto."

"Primal scream therapy." Dizzy's father Louis joined them, placing his plate in the sink. "I haven't done it in years but this just might be the time to try it. Get everything out of you. You'll feel like a new person."

Dizzy certainly wanted to scream at the top of her lungs, and her parents were inviting her to do so.

"Good idea, Louis," Tami exclaimed. "We should all do it. I'm still stressed from our hideously awful travel from overseas. Let's do it now."

Not with Zach upstairs taking a shower. He'd think a mass murder was taking place in her home. "Not now. Can you wait until I get back? We can do it then. And that meditation sounds pretty good too. I think it would help to quiet my mind."

Louis frowned at the coffee pot. "Caffeine isn't good for you, Dizzy. I hope you don't drink this often."

Only every day. It helped maintain her sunny personality.

Luckily, she didn't have to answer out loud because Zach stomped downstairs, talking into his phone. He hung up when he saw her, tucking it into his jacket pocket.

"Are you ready to go? That was Jason and they're gathering in Easton's office to wait. Our spies are saying that Trip just arrived at the police station."

Her heart accelerated and she took a slow breath. This was it. She'd been hoping and praying for the cops to talk to Trip and it was finally happening.

After bidding goodbye to her parents, who were still fussing over the coffee pot and debating the evils of caffeine, she followed Zach out to his car. Taking a backward glance at her home, she could see Tami and Louis standing at the front door waving. It was then that it hit her and she began to laugh. She hadn't even realized it until now.

"Care to share what's so funny? I could use a laugh."

"Me. I'm funny. You know, Zach, I've always thought of myself as so strange and different than everyone else. They call me eccentric and weird, and I've taken pride in that label. But this morning I realized that I'm really not anymore. Sure, I'm not what you'd call normal either but I'm not nearly as kooky and peculiar as I thought I was. Heck, I'm practically boring."

Over the years Dizzy had changed, become the person she wanted to be instead of who her parents were. All that time while she was growing up they'd cloaked their efforts by acting like they were teaching her to think for herself and not follow the crowd. But in reality, they'd wanted her to be like them.

And they had succeeded in teaching her to be an individual and think for herself, but that lesson had consequences. She wasn't going to be what they thought was right either. She'd decided to be something different. Not quite what others would call normal but not quite outlandish either. She was somewhere comfortably in the middle – happy with who she'd grown into.

Could Easton meet her somewhere in this land in between? Did he even want to?

Chapter Twenty-Nine

EASTON'S HEART WAS in his throat when Dizzy walked into his office, right behind Zach. He'd been pacing the floor waiting for her to arrive but now that she was there he didn't have a clue as to what to say or do. It wasn't his style to start a personal conversation with other people in the room and he damn well didn't need their input. He already knew their feelings about this topic. He needed to talk to Dizzy alone. Perhaps he could finagle a way after the call from the police about their questioning Trip.

Carter sidled up to Easton and leaned down to speak into his ear. "Damn, Dizzy looks good."

She did look stunning. She'd dressed for the business environment in a slim black skirt and simple white blouse. Her hair had been coiled up on top of her head but a few strands had escaped and they had the privilege of caressing her creamy pink cheeks.

"I swear to God I will beat the ever-loving shit out of you if you ask her out," Easton said between gritted teeth. "Stay away from her."

Chuckling, Carter spread his hands wide and grinned. "The

question is can she stay away from me? After all, look at me."

Easton growled at his younger brother, thoroughly frustrated and pissed off. He hadn't slept well last night without Dizzy in his bed. "I'm looking at the biggest fool in the Anderson family. Now sit the hell down and shut up."

To his surprise Carter did just that, right after snagging a coffee from the cart that his assistant had wheeled into the office. Dizzy and Leann were quietly chatting in one corner while Zach and Jason talked in another. Easton was the odd man out in this group. From the hostile waves coming off of Leann, he had a feeling he was barely being tolerated.

Walking around his desk, Jason refilled his coffee and then moved to stand by Easton.

"Are you going to apologize to Dizzy?"

"What exactly would I be apologizing for, cousin?"

"Being an asshole," Jason shot back with a smile. "In general. Seriously, just say you're sorry. I'm sure you both said things you regret."

"So I should be the one to apologize? Is that what you do? Just roll over and play dead when Brinley's pissed off?"

"If you apologize I guarantee she'll apologize as well. But if you're stubborn and want her to do it first, then you might be waiting for awhile. Or worse, you might find that she moves on to someone who doesn't need everything their way. Take some advice from an old married man...being together is more important than keeping score as to who was right and who was wrong. Keeping count is good in business but in relationships? It's petty and spiteful. Are you planning to keep track of how many kisses she gives you compared to what you give her? Are you planning to count orgasms? Hugs? Gifts? Where's the line?"

Easton didn't answer but he was already trying to digest Jason's advice. When described that way it did sound petty and nasty. But...Easton hadn't been wrong. Her parents did hate him and the Anderson family and as far as he knew that hadn't changed in the last twenty-four hours. There was also that fact that he and Dizzy were different. Of course, one of the reasons he loved being with her so much was because she wasn't a carbon copy of himself or the other women he'd dated. Leann had been right. He'd been bored with them. He needed something that so far only Dizzy had been able to give him.

All he'd asked for was a break. Was that so terrible? Was he the bad guy here?

The phone ringing had everyone whirling around to face the desk. Easton pressed a button as the group gathered around, anxious to hear any news. They were lucky that West was the mayor and that the name Anderson had influence in Tremont.

As a former law enforcement officer, Jason was taking the lead on this. "This is Jason Anderson."

"Anderson?" A male voice came over the speaker. "This is Detective Harry Larkin, West's former partner."

Ah, that's how this was happening. The detective in charge of the case was West's former partner. That's how it worked in a small town. There were only five or six detectives at any given time in Tremont so this wasn't a shock.

"Hi, Harry. Did you speak to Stanford this morning?"

Jason glanced at his watch and Easton followed suit. The conversation hadn't taken long.

"You know I shouldn't be commenting on an ongoing investigation."

Smiling, Jason nodded, although the man on the other side of the phone couldn't see him.

"I know and I appreciate your help on this. We're not planning on going to the newspaper with any of this. We just want to know if you learned anything today. I have Dizzy Foster under twenty-four-hour guard right now so I think I have a vested interest in this case. We don't want any more dead bodies in Tremont, now do we?"

"We certainly don't." The voice had a grim tone. "Listen, Stanford came in with a lawyer and refused to answer any questions on advice from counsel. We got nothing from him except now he's aroused my suspicions since he won't talk. If he's got nothing to hide, why did he lawyer up? Anyway, he was calm and nice but he wouldn't answer anything. We did warn him to stay away from Miss Foster and his lawyer said that he would."

Easton didn't trust Stanford or his attorney to leave Dizzy alone. From the expression on Jason's face it appeared his cousin agreed with that sentiment. Zach didn't look convinced either.

And Dizzy looked like she might cry. She'd had so much hope that this might move the case forward and those hopes had been crushed. Easton had to stop himself from putting his arms around her in comfort. She wouldn't welcome that.

"I appreciate that, Harry. What's your next move? We're still going to keep Miss Foster under guard here."

"We're working on getting a warrant to search Stanford's home and vehicle. Actually, you might be able to help us, Anderson. We'd like to search his office too but we'd need permission from someone at Anderson Industries. He has no expectation of privacy at his workplace."

Easton didn't hesitate for a moment. "Permission granted. How soon can you be here? I'll escort you personally."

"Wait." Leann held her hand up. "Just because he says our employees have no expectation of privacy doesn't mean that's the actual case. We need to check what's in writing at Anderson Industries."

"The law would trump our corporate policy," Easton argued, happy to see that Jason was also nodding in agreement.

"I'm not arguing about the law," Leann said. "I'm arguing that our employees have a level of trust with management. We can't just allow the police to search someone's office if we've said that is something that we wouldn't allow. If we don't have a policy regarding this or we say that they have no expectations, then fine. But if we do...I think we need to have a warrant before we allow them in. I know this is personal for us but we have to look at the bigger picture."

"I don't want you to do anything that's unethical," Dizzy declared, nervously tugging at the strap on her handbag. Funny how after only a few weeks he knew her well enough to notice her little gestures. "I don't want Trip to be able to get off on a technicality either."

Giving in gracefully, Easton shrugged. "Then we'll have to get back to you, Harry. Give me an hour and I'll go through our employee handbook with a fine tooth comb."

Although it looked like Leann was already on it, tapping furiously into her phone.

Jason bid the detective goodbye and hung up. "Well, I can't say that I'm shocked that Stanford lawyered up. If he were stupid he would have already been caught. At least Harry is now suspicious. Hopefully they can get that warrant."

"And if they can't?" Dizzy asked, her expression stormy. This had to be the hardest on her. She was still in danger and Easton didn't know what to say or do to make it all better. He'd only made it worse.

"Then they'll find another way," Zach replied, confidence in his tone. "He'll mess up eventually. They all do."

The meeting broke up and Zach pulled Easton aside in the hallway. "I just wanted to let you know that Jason and I talked about this morning and we're going to put a twenty-four-hour guard outside of Dizzy's house as well as me staying there. I'm going to stay put in Tremont until we get some resolution on this."

Easton appreciated what Zach was doing but the truth was *he* wanted to be the one helping and protecting Dizzy. They needed to talk about things and now would be a good time for that. Maybe he could take her out for a cup of coffee and a Danish.

"Thanks, Zach. I know that you're doing your best and I appreciate the extra manpower. Hopefully once Dizzy and I sit down and talk I'll be back and able to give you a hand."

"It's good news that you're going to work things out."

"I'm planning to ask her for coffee." Easton looked back into the office but it was empty. "I didn't see her leave."

Shifting on his feet, Zach tugged at the collar of his buttoned-down shirt. "She and Leann walked right past us when we came out here. I think they left."

Okay, he couldn't ask her for coffee. Time to go to Plan B. Whatever that was.

Chapter Thirty

D IZZY SWUNG OUT of the passenger side of Leann's car. During the drive, she'd bounced back and forth between angry and happy while Leann tried to be the voice of reason. The problem was Dizzy didn't want to be reasonable; she wanted to be mad or glad. Dammit, she was so confused she didn't know what she wanted other than chocolate and lots of it.

She was frustrated that Trip had lawyered up.

Relieved that the police were finally taking her seriously.

Angry that Easton had looked so calm and cool.

Happy that she'd managed to keep her dignity in front of him.

"Thank you for driving me home. I do appreciate it. I made some chocolate chip cookies. How about a couple and a cup of coffee? Or do you need to get back to the office?"

"I would never turn one of your baked goods down. Anderson can do without me for a little while."

They entered the house and dropped their purses on the kitchen table. The back door was wide open so Tami and Louis must have been in the backyard enjoying the day. It was a bit chilly but the sun made the weather quite comfortable.

Dizzy headed straight for the coffee pot. "I'll get the coffee going–"

Leann's gasp had her whirling around to see what had shocked her friend so badly that she was standing in the doorway, her face white as a sheet.

"What's wrong?" Dizzy looked out the back door and groaned, wanting to dig a hole in the backyard and bury herself, never to be seen again. Her parents had two yoga mats on the back lawn.

They were doing yoga.

In the nude.

Currently they were in Downward Facing Dog.

Dizzy was pretty sure Leann would never do yoga again. If she didn't gouge out her eyes out on the spot.

"I'm going to have to move," Dizzy muttered under her breath, making a beeline for Tami and Louis. What were they thinking? This was the suburbs, not their former old house in the boonies. There were laws about indecent exposure.

"Tami! Louis! You can't do that out here!" Dizzy grabbed their robes hung on the porch railing on her way. "For heaven's sake, cover up before my neighbors call the police."

Tami and Louis rose to their feet and didn't look a bit repentant. They also didn't put on their robes.

"We were just letting go of our stress," Tami explained. "It's therapy."

"You're naked," Dizzy shot back. "This is a family neighborhood and you can't walk around *naked* in it. People don't like that. I'm serious about this. You need to go out somewhere deserted for that."

"People should mind their own business," Louis said with a huff. "If they don't like what they see, they can turn away."

People were going to need a bottle of eye bleach and a therapist.

"The human body is a work of art," Tami argued, finally shrugging into the robe that Dizzy was holding out for her. "It's meant to be displayed, not hidden. We taught you not to be ashamed of your body."

"And I'm not, but other people don't have the same ideas, and we have to respect the way other people think and believe, right? You can do yoga *inside* the house."

Preferably when Dizzy wasn't at home. The human body was a beautiful work of art but it was a little weird to see her parents naked. She'd never been comfortable with it even when she was younger and didn't realize nudity was a thing.

"Society is so judgmental," her mother said, shaking her head in disappointment. "And now our daughter is too. This is a sad day."

Dizzy wasn't sure of much these days but she was definitely sure that she wasn't going to take any crap from her parents about being judgmental. Breezing past them, she headed to the kitchen with Leann in tow. "Yes, that's the problem with society today. We're judgmental. Except that you're judging them for judging you."

Leann quietly took a seat at the kitchen table as Dizzy reached for the box of coffee filters in the cabinet but her countertop didn't look quite right. It took her a moment to realize that her coffee pot was missing.

It was the last straw.

She'd take their crappy comments about her life and her stress and her friends. But they were not going to take her caffeinated buddy. They'd gone too far this time.

Whirling around, she marched right up to them, anger churning in her gut. Whenever she was mad she cried and she didn't want to do that this time. Her parents needed to know she was pissed as hell.

She could feel how red her face was by the heat under her skin. She was literally shaking with rage. "Where is my coffee-maker?"

Tami and Louis looked at each other and smiled. Like this was a happy occasion. *Fools*. Her father stepped forward. "Caffeine is not good for you when you're under stress, pumpkin. We'll replace it with a nice juice machine. You can juice fruits and vegetables. Much healthier. We'll run into town today and buy one."

She'd heard about people seeing red but she'd never realized that a person actually could indeed see red. Yet, here she was with a red haze in front of her eyes. Too bad she hadn't had it a few minutes ago when they were naked in her backyard. "Put it back."

"Now, Dizzy," Tami began, but Dizzy was having none of it.

"Put it back now," she hissed. She knew good and well this was about more than the coffee pot, but did they?

Tami frowned and shook her head. "This is why you're so tense."

Dizzy's fingers furled into fists and with all the emotions that she had whirring inside of her frustration was the winner.

"I'm tense because I witnessed my neighbor strangling a

woman and hardly anyone in this town believes me." Dizzy's voice was rising with every other word. "And do you know why they don't believe me? Because I'm different and weird. But I learned something since you got here. I'm really not that strange. I'm more like them than I am like you. I bet that doesn't make you happy, does it?"

That question was said in a whisper after all the yelling. She didn't know whether she was coming or going anymore. She was just so confused as to how she was supposed to be feeling. She only knew two things for sure. One, that Trip needed to be brought to justice, and two, that she was probably in love with Easton. Everything else was a blur.

Just like that these two people weren't annoying or trouble-some or making her insane. They were her parents and Tami's arms were open wide. Dizzy flew into them with a sob, letting her mother stroke her hair and whisper soft words of encouragement. Louis, who prided himself on being a male in touch with his feminine side, joined in, dropping a kiss on the top of her head and making silly faces. He used to do that when she was a child and she'd skinned her knee. She'd end up giggling while her mother cleaned the wound and applied a Band-aid.

"Um, I think I better go. I have a meeting I forgot all about."

Leann had inched her way to the door and looked ready to flee. Dizzy didn't blame her a bit. The Foster family was in a three-alarm crisis and she was sure she didn't want to witness or be a part of it.

"Thank you for bringing Dizzy home," Tami said. "Sorry about the coffee."

Leann muttered something like *no problem* and then zipped

out of the door.

"Thank you for being nice to Leann," Dizzy said in between sniffles. Her cheeks were damp from crying and she hated crying. She'd done it far too often lately. "You weren't nice to Easton."

"We're the same that we've always been," Tami said. "You're the one that's changed."

Dizzy opened her mouth to defend herself but her mother shook her head and continued.

"It's not a bad thing. It's just different. We're not disappointed. We love you, Dizzy. We just want you to be happy."

"Easton makes me happy."

Her parents exchanged a glance that Dizzy couldn't decipher but Louis didn't keep her in suspense. "Then that's all we need to know. We admit that he isn't what we pictured, pumpkin, but if he's what you want then that's what we want for you."

That statement couldn't have been easy for her parents to make and they didn't look happy about saying it, but they also didn't look like they were going to argue, either.

"It doesn't matter anyway." She hiccupped as a fresh spate of tears began. "Easton and I broke up."

"Because of us."

The way Tami said it didn't make it sound like a question.

"Yes, he hates the idea that you don't like him or his family. He's proud to be an Anderson and rightly so."

Louis's brows shot up. "So you just gave up? Let him walk away? That doesn't sound like my little pumpkin. She would have fought for what she wanted. Maybe you don't care about him as much as you think you do. Maybe it's just the sex."

Heat rushed into her cheeks and she wished the earth would

open up and swallow her. She did not want this conversation with her parents. "It's not just the sex."

Her mother shrugged and tapped her chin. "He is a sexy man, and he has big feet too. Any girl would want to get into his pants. But looks aren't everything, you know. The real question is does he know what to do with his–"

"Tami! Please stop. I will say I haven't missed this."

Dizzy buried her face in her hands, completely mortified.

"I'm just saying that there's more to a man than his looks." Her mother was chuckling and so was Louis. "Young people these days are so prudish. Sex is a perfectly normal biological need, and I'm assuming our daughter is not a virgin."

Not even close but that wasn't the point.

She didn't raise her head from her hands, preferring not to look her parents in the eye. Not today. Maybe not tomorrow, either.

"Please let's not talk about sex."

"Fine," Tami huffed. "What do you want to talk about? How wimpy you are? How you let life happen to you instead of going after what you want?"

Dizzy's head jerked up and her eyes widened. "That's a crappy thing to say. You're parents. You're supposed to try and make me feel better about myself. You're supposed to build my self-esteem."

"That's exactly what we're doing," Louis replied with a grin, wrapping his arm around his wife.

"What crazy kind of ABC Afterschool Special is this? I'm not feeling all that great about myself when you call me wimpy."

"Then do something about it," Tami answer promptly. "Or

you can stay here and be miserable."

"I don't want to be miserable," she answered automatically.

"And you want Easton." Her mother's gaze ran over her daughter. "And yet here you are blaming us for losing him when you could be with him working things out."

It was a little their fault but she and Easton had a whole lot of ownership in this argument too.

"I don't blame you—"

"Lovely," Tami said, pushing her toward the door. "Now go get him. I don't want to hear you cry about him for the next fifty or sixty years and on into your next reincarnation. Go work this out. Your father and I still have more primal screaming therapy, plus we're not done with our nude yoga. Unless you'd rather give up on Easton and join us. Your father's favorite is the Eagle pose. It's good for his sciatica."

Oh hell no.

Dizzy was going to need to bake cookies for the entire cul de sac after her parents left to apologize. For the screaming. For the nudity. And anything else her parents might think up between now and then.

Retrieving her purse from the table by the door, Dizzy dug for her car keys. "I'm going to talk to him."

"Have fun and make sure he sees to your sexual needs as much as his own, pumpkin," her father said with a wave. "We love you."

They did. She was sure of it.

"I love you too."

After the strangest pep talk ever, she was ready to go work things out with Easton. She was ready to admit that she loved him. He might love her or he might not but he cared, and that was a start. Time to take this Anderson bull by the horns and get her man.

This wasn't about her parents. Or what they believed or what she believed. This was about the two of them scared to death and getting cold feet. Time to warm up those toes.

It was time to be happy.

Chapter Thirty-One

E ASTON'S ASSISTANT STOOD in the doorway of his office just as he was gathering his notes for an important meeting with his brother Shane. They needed to make some decisions regarding a few upcoming projects.

"Whoever it is tell them I'll call them back. I was supposed to be in the boardroom five minutes ago."

Amy had a strange smile on her face and her cheeks were pink with excitement. He didn't remember the last time she looked this animated.

"Are you sure? Because there's a young woman here to see you. She says it's important."

Sighing with frustration, he counted to three before replying. Amy was too good of an assistant to yell at over something trivial. It wasn't her fault he was in a lousy mood and hadn't had enough sleep last night.

"It being important doesn't make me any less late," Easton explained. "Have her make an appointment."

That smile grew annoyingly wider. "Okay, I'll just tell Dizzy that you're too busy to see her."

Dizzy? Here?

"Wait," he barked, dropping his notes on the desk as his heart leapt into his throat and his stomach plummeted to his feet. "Dizzy's here?"

Amy nodded and Easton could swear she giggled too. "She is. Should I send her in after all?"

Straightening his tie, he took a deep breath but it failed to slow his racing pulse. Why had she come? What did it matter? He could fix this now. "Yes, please and let Shane know that I'll be delayed."

Amy whirled on her heel and marched out of the office. "Will do, Boss."

It felt like forever waiting for Dizzy to enter his office but it was actually only a few seconds. She was still dressed in that sexy black skirt and white blouse, her legs looking amazing in black high-heeled pumps. At some point, her hair had fallen out of its up-do and it was now lying in a riot of chocolate waves around her shoulders.

"I hope this isn't a bad time."

Clearing his throat so he could speak, he motioned to the small sofa on the right side of his office. "It's fine. Please have a seat."

They both sat on the soft leather couch with a respectable ten to twelve inches between them. Easton's fingers itched to reach out and touch the soft skin of her cheek but at this point he didn't dare. He hoped she was here to work things out but maybe she was just there to bring him a pair of socks he'd forgotten and had ended up in her laundry.

She looked as nervous as he felt, her hands wrung together so tightly the knuckles were white. She hadn't looked at him, not fully, and now his own nerves had kicked in. She was probably there to tell him she never wanted to see him again.

"I'm very sorry about what my parents said," she began, her gaze still on her hands. "They're challenging and they have some very definite ideas about things. Like screaming, yoga and nudity."

Um…okay. He wasn't quite following here.

"Yoga?"

She finally looked up and their gazes met. Her brown eyes were dark with emotion – maybe sadness or regret?

"And nudity," she confirmed. "Just ask Leann. I'll probably be paying for her therapy bills for awhile."

What in the hell had happened in the last hour and a half? Leann had looked just fine this morning.

"She's a licensed clinical therapist, Dizzy. I'm sure she can handle whatever it is."

"That's not why I came here." Dizzy lifted her chin and reached across the space between them to place her hand on his. Her skin so incredibly soft and warm. His own fingers wound through hers and she didn't pull away. A good sign. "I came here because I want to say that I'm sorry–"

"No," he interrupted hastily. This wasn't the way it was supposed to go. "No, I'm the one that's sorry, baby. I intended to come see you tonight. I'm the one that screwed up and I'm the one that needs to apologize. I am really sorry, Dizzy. I acted like a jerk and you were right to throw my ass out. If you're willing to keep seeing me despite how your parents feel then I should simply count myself lucky. Hopefully someday they will change their minds but in the meantime, I want to make you the happiest woman in Tremont. I...I love you, honey."

Her entire body seemed to relax and she slumped against the cushions. "I came here to apologize for telling you to go fuck yourself. I love you too."

His heart seemed far too large for his chest, making it hard to take a breath. She loved him too. He'd almost screwed this up completely but somehow she'd forgiven him.

"I was scared," he confessed, pulling her closer so he could feel the warmth of her skin and smell the floral fragrance of her hair. "Your parents reminded me of how different we were and I thought you would eventually get bored with me. I'm so bland compared to you."

He pressed his lips to her forehead and she looked up at him and smiled. There was a love and tenderness in her face that he'd never seen before, and he wanted to see it every day, all the time.

"You don't bore me in the least. And it turns out that I might not be as different and strange as I thought. I might be almost as normal as you are. Let's not tell anyone."

There was a story behind this but now was definitely not the time to find out about it. He'd rather kiss her instead. Besides, he could never think of her as merely normal. She was everything that he wasn't and more. He wouldn't have her any other way, either.

Pressing her back onto the cushions of the sofa, his lips found the spot where her pulse beat madly at the base of her throat before traveling up her neck to linger behind her ear. Her hands, however, were pushing at his chest and slightly dazed, he lifted himself up.

"Do you want me to stop?"

He would if she wanted him to, of course. His office wasn't the most romantic place for a reunion.

Her smile was sexy and inviting, and her fingers were trailing down his chest to his stomach.

"I want you to lock the door."

She was as brilliant as she was beautiful.

Chapter Thirty-Two

EASTON HAD MANAGED to wrap up work early and take Dizzy to the diner for a bite to eat. She was proud of him leaving the office before it was dark and she'd teased him that perhaps he should make a habit of it.

Their afternoon lovemaking had made both of them ravenous and before she knew it they'd demolished cheeseburgers and fries, practically doing everything but licking their plates clean. Patting her very full stomach, Dizzy sat back and sighed with contentment.

"Nobody makes better burgers than this place," she said. "This was totally worth blowing off a couple of meetings for. Admit it."

"It is nice, but you know I can't do this every day. But I'm definitely going to try to do it more often."

That was good enough for her. She didn't need Easton every minute of the day. She just wanted to make sure that he made their relationship a priority.

"Do you mind if I run next door for a minute? I want to see if Carla got anything new in."

It was only one door down and there would be other people.

She'd be fine.

"I'm sure she has." Easton pulled out his credit card to pay the check. "Go ahead and I'll be there in a minute. I wouldn't mind picking up something new either."

Sliding out of the booth, she dashed over to the bookstore, waving at Carla as she entered, heading straight for the cozy mystery section. There appeared to be a few new titles on the table. One had a delicious-looking cupcake on the cover and it appeared to be a new book in a series she'd enjoyed. She picked it up to read the back to make sure it wasn't one she'd already read but with a new cover.

"Funny running into you here."

A familiar voice pulled her from her reading and she whirled around to find herself face to face with Trip Stanford. Far too close. He'd violated social norms of personal space by being only a few inches from her but she didn't dare take a step back and let him know that his proximity bothered her.

She wouldn't give him the satisfaction.

"Trip."

She didn't have anything else to say. She didn't care if he was having a nice day or what he was reading or how he'd been, so acting like she did would be the height of hypocrisy.

Trip leaned down to look at the cover of her book. "That looks like a good one. A murder mystery, eh? You must really like those."

The douchebag was smirking. *Smirking.* Looking far too pleased with himself.

She held up the paperback, her stomach churning with a mixture of anger and disgust. No, make that fury. He looked so superior as if he had the world in his pocket.

"They always get the killer in the end, although it might take a little time. But they always do."

"Books are like that. Real life is different."

Not this time, asshole.

"Not so different. Killers are caught every day."

He tapped the book with his finger. "Maybe you should stick with stories, Dizzy. Make-believe and fairy tales."

Her fingers tightened on the book and for a moment she contemplated smacking him upside the head with it but she'd been brought up not to consider violence an answer. But she was seriously questioning her upbringing right about now.

"I know what's real and what isn't," she said instead, fighting to keep her tone even despite the rage that was sweeping through her at his smug attitude. "And I know what I saw. I'm not about to forget it."

He smiled like a man that didn't have a care in the world. "You need to let it go."

"I won't."

"You should. No one believes you." Leaning forward, he chuckled and his voice dropped to a whisper. "I got away with it."

The bell over the door rang and Easton strode into the bookstore, his gaze scanning the back of the room for her. When it found her, his expression turned thunderous and even Trip took a few steps backward. He might mess with her but he clearly didn't want to tangle with Easton Anderson.

With a strong arm wrapped around Dizzy's waist, Easton glowered at Trip. "Stanford. You're off work a little early."

"I took a vacation day." Trip wasn't smirking anymore but he was still smiling. "I had a few things to take care of."

Easton smiled as well but it wasn't a real one. "Yes, I heard the police brought you in this morning for questioning. You lawyered up. Probably a smart move on your part."

"You can't be too careful. The judicial system can easily railroad an innocent man."

Dizzy couldn't take this bullshit anymore.

"You just admitted you got away with it."

Trip feigned outrage, his eyes going comically wide and his mouth falling open.

"I certainly did no such thing. You really need to stop making up stories, Dizzy. I wouldn't hurt a fly."

Easton rubbed his chin and nodded. "That's good to hear because when I was paying the check at the diner I got a call from my cousin West. He still has contacts in the police department and he told me that the search warrants for your home, vehicle, and office have all been approved by the judge. If you hurry home now, you might just have time to move your victim's body off of your property before the cops get there."

That smug look was wiped away completely, leaving a pale and shaken man. Trip quickly turned on his heel and raced out of the bookstore leaving Dizzy and Easton behind. She sagged against for support, her emotions taking every ounce of energy she'd had left.

"Please tell me what you said was true," she pleaded.

"Part of it was true."

"Which part? Did they only get a warrant for the office or something?"

"No, they got the warrants for his house, car, and office. The part that wasn't true was that he had time to move the body." Easton smiled then. A gleeful smile. "They're already at his house. You did it, baby. You got him."

This wasn't about Dizzy, though. This was justice for Janine Erskine, who might rest a little more in peace after today.

✦ ✦ ✦

EASTON AND DIZZY stood off to the side of Trip's driveway as Janine's body was rolled on a gurney from the backyard to the front. She was shrouded in a body bag but that didn't stop his stomach twisting in his abdomen as she was loaded into the coroner's van.

It was all so sad and wasteful. Trip had killed that poor girl when she should have had a long life ahead of her. Maybe a husband and kids. Or at least that cat she wanted to adopt. There wouldn't be any of that now. All because Trip couldn't control his anger toward women.

Of course, Trip hadn't made it home before the cops had begun their search. He'd been handcuffed while they dug up his flowerbed and scoured his home. His truck had been impounded. Bag after bag of evidence had streamed out of the backyard, carried by crime scene investigators dressed in jumpsuits and wearing gloves. At one point, West had shown up and spoken to the lead detective before coming to stand beside Easton and Dizzy.

"He's not saying anything without his lawyer," West reported, a grim expression on his face. "But he did say he wanted a deal. Says he has some information about a missing girl in

Washington State."

The acrid taste of bile rose in Easton's throat. Trip had been so sure he'd gotten away with it. Was this the second time? Zach was sure that Trip wasn't a practiced killer but that didn't mean Janine was his first.

"I think he'd say anything right about now," Dizzy replied softly, so low he could barely hear her.

None of them were happy. There was no triumph, no elation at Trip's arrest. There was a woman who was dead that shouldn't be. And it had only been an accident of fate that Dizzy had witnessed it.

Or maybe there was more to it. Maybe it was that crazy universe at work that Dizzy always talked about. Was her standing there at that exact moment something more? Certainly there was evil in the world, but there was goodness as well. Who was to say that each side didn't have an army in that never-ending battle? If Easton had to choose someone to fight the good fight he would certainly select Dizzy. She was formidable and she'd never given up, even when the odds were against her.

Sergeant Baker, the cop that had patronized Dizzy that first night, stepped out of the house and down the front steps, stopping in front of the three of them. He shuffled his feet and cleared his throat.

"I just want to say, Miss Foster, that I'm real sorry I didn't take you seriously that night. I should have and that's my mistake."

At first Easton thought Dizzy wasn't going to reply and he wouldn't have blamed her. There were a whole bunch of Tremont residents that were going to be eating a heaping helping of crow tonight. But eventually she did and her eyes were bright with tears as she gripped Easton's arm.

"Apology accepted. Just take good care of Janine, okay? She deserves our best."

The sergeant's throat bobbed and his cheeks turned red, but he nodded in agreement.

"We're going to do right by her, Miss Foster. I promise."

The sergeant walked away and West drifted off as well to speak to one of the detectives. Easton leaned down to drop a brief kiss on her cheek, salty from her tears.

"I'm so proud of you, baby. You never gave up, never took no for an answer. Even from me. The universe picked the perfect warrior for this battle."

Her lips quirked up into a smile. "Easton Anderson, are you admitting that perhaps there might be things that are true and real that you can't see?"

He wanted to spend the rest of his life with this woman. Nope, make that all of his lives. He and Dizzy were destined to be together.

"Yes, I am."

Chapter Thirty-Three

TAMI FOSTER ACCEPTED the glass of wine from Easton's mother Kathy. Their husbands were chatting away next to them about the merits of private versus public school education. To her surprise, it sounded like they actually agreed.

Of course, it was going to be a few years before Easton and Dizzy's children attended school. Her daughter had only been dating Easton for a few weeks but clearly, they were head over heels for each other. That was why she and Louis had agreed to come to Sunday dinner at the Anderson home. They'd better get to know their soon-to-be in-laws a little better. Sure, she'd spent some time with Kathy and Joe through the years but they were going to be family, and that was a whole other kettle of fish.

The two couples were standing at the kitchen sink looking out of the window at Easton and Dizzy kissing in the gazebo. They really were a sweet couple and the boy had already begun growing on Tami. Anyone who loved Dizzy that much had to be a good man.

Kathy sighed, her smile growing wider as they watched the couple snuggle together on the gazebo bench. They appeared to be whispering and giggling about something, probably sex, but

Tami didn't say it out loud.

"Do you think we can have a spring wedding?" Kathy asked, turning to Tami. "Or maybe June? That's a lovely month for a wedding."

"We can be back from Greece by then," Louis agreed readily. "That gives the kids time to plan it."

"I'd like three or four grandchildren," Tami declared. "Two boys and two girls. What about you, Kathy?"

Chuckling, Kathy took a sip of her wine. "That sounds good, although after raising four boys I wouldn't mind all girls."

Joe shook his head. "Now ladies, Easton hasn't even proposed and you're planning weddings and babies. We have to let them do it at their pace."

"I could give them a little push," Tami suggested. "I think in our travels we picked up a few witchcraft books. I could cast a spe–"

Louis looked appalled. "Good God, woman, no. With your luck, you'd end up conjuring a demon and set it loose on the whole town."

Her husband was always so dramatic. She would have been careful.

Kathy sniffed disdainfully. "It might just be what Tremont deserves for not believing Dizzy. Now I don't believe in witchcraft but I do believe in the magic of that gazebo. We'll have a wedding within the year. I guarantee it."

Tami held up her wine glass. "I'll drink to that. To our children's future, love and babies. To becoming a family."

All four of them clinked glasses and Tami saw the sun begin to peek through the gray clouds that had been hanging over them all day. Maybe the universe was listening after all.

Love would always triumph in the end.

I hope you enjoyed Easton and Dizzy's happily ever after!
Look for Carter's story in 2018!

Thank you for reading Window to Danger!

Don't miss a thing! Sign up to be notified of Olivia's new releases:

oliviajaymesoptin.instapage.com

About The Author

Olivia Jaymes is a wife, mother, lover of sexy romance, and caffeine addict. She lives with her husband and son in central Florida and spends her days with handsome alpha males and spunky heroines.

She is currently working on a new contemporary romance series – The Hollywood Showmance Chronicles in addition to the ongoing Danger Incorporated series.

Visit Olivia Jaymes at

www.OliviaJaymes.com

Other Titles by Olivia Jaymes

Danger Incorporated
Damsel In Danger
Hiding From Danger
Discarded Heart Novella
Indecent Danger
Embracing Danger
Danger In The Night
Reunited With Danger

Cowboy Justice Association
Cowboy Command
Justice Healed
Cowboy Truth
Cowboy Famous
Cowboy Cool
Imperfect Justice
The Deputies
Justice Inked
Justice Reborn
Vengeful Justice

Military Moguls
Champagne and Bullets

Diamonds and Revolvers

Caviar and Covert Ops

Emeralds, Rubies, and Camouflage

Midnight Blue Beach
Wicked After Midnight

Midnight Of No Return

Kiss Midnight Goodbye

The Hollywood Showmance Chronicles
A Kiss For the Cameras

Swinging From A Star